A QUIET GENOCIDE

THE UNTOLD HOLOCAUST OF DISABLED CHILDREN IN WW2 GERMANY

GLENN BRYANT

For Juliet Robson, a UK artist whose work and spirit inspired this story

'We have broken the laws of natural selection. We have supported unworthy life forms and we have allowed them to breed.' (Adolf Hitler, 1925)

CHAPTER ONE

Breakfast was business-like in the Diederich household. Catharina asked Gerhard what time he would be home from work and what he would prefer for supper. Gerhard was polite and accommodating in response, but cradling a hangover the size of a U-boat he was in no mood to upset. He was a skilled man from the upper working class and he had married above his modest station when he and Catharina had fallen in love at a dance in Munich in the summer of 1929. Twenty-five winters had passed since. It had been a quick courtship and they had wed in December that year. Catharina's father was a casualty of the Great War and her once comfortable family were on hard times. Gerhard had steady work in interwar Germany, which few peers did, and even though Catharina's mother was fighting disappointed tears on their wedding day – a cold but clear day – in the circumstances he was a decent match, dependable.

Catharina had taken odd jobs but she had never consistently worked. The soft hands she used to stroke the face of Jozef, their only child, revealed as much. She ran a good house, she was a dutiful wife, she was a doting mother and she was stunning. But age was starting to creep up on her, invisible like the tide, which alarmed her if she ever caught her reflection in a weak moment.

Catharina's friends from her youth and their strictly middle-class husbands peered down on Gerhard, as if they were removing their reading glasses reproachfully before bringing him sharply into focus. They were all doing worse when it came to money in their pockets, but, perversely, rampant inflation and an economic crash had only made them cling more stubbornly to their status and increased the number of jibes.

Tonight, Gerhard and Catharina were hosting the parents of their son's closest friend, Sebastian, for dinner. Gerhard was drained from drinking the previous night and he really did not care to, but Catharina maintained it was good etiquette given the fact that their sons spent so much time together. Sebastian's parents, Karl and Jana, enjoyed these occasions more, but only when they entertained. Jana was a much better cook than Catharina, who knew it.

A warm knock at the front door. Karl and Jana.

Jozef was quickest and paced down the Diederich's narrow hallway. He opened the door into darkness and rain and, more happily, Karl and Jana and Sebastian smiling.

'Jozef!' said Jana. 'How handsome you look.'

'Thank you Frau Gottlieb,' he replied.

'Jana, please Jozef,' said Jana, briefly touching his hair.

Jozef's mother walked up the hallway, wiping her wet hands on a tea towel. 'Jana, how are you?' she said kindly, brushing over any discomfort between them and wondering why they did not have the Gottliebs over more often. She liked it. It was sociable. It was pleasant.

The two women kissed each other tenderly on the cheek.

'Gerhard,' said Karl more formally, shaking Gerhard's hand through the crowd. 'Come through, come through,' he said, desperately trying to perk himself up. Tonight felt like completing back-to-back shifts in the office. He had to be on duty. A drink would help dull that depression, he thought. 'Let me take your coats,' he said, heaping them up on overcrowded hooks in the hallway.

'What can I get you both to drink?' asked his wife. 'Wine? We only have red I'm afraid but you can have whisky with Gerhard if you prefer, Karl.'

'Wine will be perfect,' said Karl.

'We only drink red anyway,' added Jana, lying politely.

Karl, Jana and Gerhard filled the Diederich's front room, tidied immaculately by Catharina earlier in the day.

Gerhard noticed the effort she had made. He remained in a dated brown work suit but he had removed his tie, while Karl wore an elegant crisp white shirt with two buttons undone at the top. It was clear he was still slim, desirable. Jana was in a beautiful, sweeping blue dress, cut confidently above her calves, and high heels, which she playfully removed. Gerhard could not help peeking at her shapely legs and neat feet with painted toenails when she did so. Jana did not notice. Karl didn't miss the moment, but let it pass.

The wine and whisky worked kindly, softening the atmosphere while candlelight flattered people's flaws with its flicker.

With Catharina in and out of the room completing final preparations for dinner, talk turned to the war and twelve years of National Socialist rule in Germany.

'I was never that enthusiastic about that moustache,' said Jana, half smiling until she saw no one was replying in kind.

'I remember once paying four million Deutsche Marks for sausages and bread,' Karl said quickly to save his wife's dignity. 'I think we all thought democracy had failed.'

Gerhard was more drunk than anyone else in the room. Intoxication started to loosen his tongue. He was aroused by Jana's presence at their table.

Catharina had not realised what state he was in, but she knew her husband was drinking quickly and she tensed every time he opened his mouth, fearing what might fall out.

'Brutality is respected in this world,' he said too casually for comfort. 'People needed something to fear. They wanted to be frightened.'

'You sound like you miss him,' teased Jana, trying to make light of his stance.

'There was enormous poverty at the time,' said Catharina quickly and uncharacteristically, because she nearly always hid her true thoughts. 'But what I think really helped Hitler was the way French soldiers humiliated people.'

Karl nodded in agreement and Catharina was eternally grateful and breathed more easily again. Karl was sipping red wine and enjoying the main course of steak and boiled potatoes. His steak was dry, but it was a good cut of meat and he was touched by the expense Catharina had gone to.

'I remember French troops beating people for using the pavement,' he said. 'They used riding crops.'

Karl heard one of the boys fall with a thud upstairs, followed by guilty giggles.

'Boys?' called Jana loudly over her shoulder.

'Yes, mother,' answered Sebastian.

'Settle down.'

'Yes, Frau Gottlieb,' said Jozef.

'Call me Jana, please.'

Gerhard winced at her last statement. It was too liberal for his conservative tastes and he immediately cooled.

'I disliked Hitler when he spoke,' said Catharina, delighted disaster had so far been averted. 'He was always shouting.'

'He was observing me,' said Gerhard, who had a drunken distance fixed on his face.

'Have you both finished?' Catharina quickly turned to her guests, desperate to cut her husband off. She rose impatiently to her feet.

'Yes, we have,' said Jana, sensing something was wrong. 'It was lovely – truly. We haven't had steak for so long. It was a wonderful treat.'

I bet you have steak every night, you stupid cow, thought Gerhard.

Catharina smiled unconvincingly and carried the plates through to the kitchen.

Gerhard began again, 'He was observing me. I felt his eyes resting on me. It was the most curious moment of my life.'

'You met Hitler?' said Jana, incredulous.

'Yes,' said Gerhard, refocusing on reality and the people around him. 'At a rally in Nuremberg in 1933. I was with our friend Michael, who you might remember arranged for us to adopt Jozef.'

Karl and Jana knew Jozef was adopted, but any mention of it made them uneasy and they held their tongues, waiting for Gerhard to finish and be done with the subject. They wished they hadn't brought it up. They should have known better.

'Hitler stared straight through me,' said Gerhard. 'An unknowable distance. I was convinced then.'

In the kitchen, Catharina's pile of dirty plates and cutlery suddenly felt leaden.

'I was convinced then,' repeated Gerhard. 'Hitler was a man of honourable intentions. I saw his wonderful side and no one can take that away from me.'

Karl and Jana did not know what to think.

In the kitchen Catharina mechanically prepared a modest dessert of peaches and milk. Gerhard poured himself another drink.

CHAPTER TWO

Michael came around every Thursday.

Jozef soon worked out the weekly visits were timed to avoid his mother, who had choir practice that evening in town. She often did not return until late after enjoying some gossip with the other singers. She knew Michael came. It was no secret. Occasionally the pair surprised each other on opposing paths in the Diederich's doorway. Michael managed those moments best, politely greeting Catharina, who quickly returned the compliment, but who avoided eye contact and hastily escaped his more confident presence. Gerhard was always pleased to see Michael. They hugged like old friends, but Jozef did not know where from.

Michael sported round spectacles, like a teacher who had taught for 1,000 years. He always brought Jozef one glass bottle of Coca-Cola and one bar of chocolate. Jozef suspected it was an act of bribery, but he did not care. Michael seemed kind.

Michael and Gerhard talked non-stop those evenings in the Diederich's front room, accompanied by the wireless and savouring Gerhard's best whisky. Jozef noticed his father only shared his most expensive liquor with Michael. Even at Christmas, the cheap bottle came out for close relatives.

The pair smoked cigarettes but less than they drank. Still, by the end of the evening the space was filled with a fog echoing Bavaria in the Middle Ages. Jozef sat respectfully apart, but he loved inhaling the rare clouds that floated his way and experiencing the rushes of nicotine. The men often became quite drunk, but Michael always retained a certain style and certain quality. Michael never appeared drunk and Jozef had never witnessed him lose his calm, warm demeanour, unlike his father, who could quickly become ill-tempered and emotional when inebriated.

'How are things Jozef? And how is school?' Michael asked this evening. He was standing over Jozef in the doorway, with his hand resting protectively on top of his shoulder.

Jozef felt its power. 'Gut Michael. Danke,' he said, remaining on his best behaviour.

'Herr Drescher to you, young man,' warned his father.

'Gerhard, we are all equals here this evening,' corrected Michael and Gerhard did not argue.

'And how is school Jozef?' Michael repeated, leading the three of them through to the Diederich's neat but modest front room, taking off his coat and expensive scarf and placing them on the side of the armchair he always favoured.

'Gut danke Herr Drescher,' Jozef remembered.

Gerhard had two generous glasses of whisky poured and waiting on a beaten and faded coffee table. The decanter of alcohol breathed in air at its centre. Jozef felt he could say anything on these occasions.

'If you are ever in trouble at school, you must tell your father, promise me that,' said Michael. 'You are special, Jozef.'

The next morning, the first snow of the winter blanketed Munich, pure and thick. Every crunching step was like devouring the world's most divine potato chip, thought Jozef, plotting a path to Sebastian's house and then school.

'Jozef!' cried Sebastian, sprinting out his front door.

Jozef had only a moment to glance up before a snowball thudded against his breast. He immediately bent down to make and hurl one himself. The two friends clanged happily into one another like pots and pans on the path leading up the hill from Sebastian's house. The snow had brightened everyone's outlook. Ruined, bombed houses looked elegant even in white, like Hitler had never happened for a day.

Jozef went overboard and shoulder charged Sebastian, bowling his companion over into someone's front garden. Sebastian picked himself up from the now flawed carpet, but not without first making a snowball to fire back in retaliation.

'Get off my fucking lawn!' complained a voice.

Jozef and Sebastian froze and despite the breathless chill flushed hot. The top half of an unkempt man, unshaven and topless but for a grubby white vest, was poking out the front door, only a few yards from the boys. They turned and desperately ran and ran until they felt safe again and began laughing.

'What an arse!' said Jozef.

'I know!' said Sebastian. 'What's wrong with him?'

Jozef and Sebastian both had double German first thing that day in school. It flew by and carried them all the way to the mid-morning break. Herr Slupski took it and was something of a maverick and their favourite teacher at school by far. Pupils vied for his attention and they cherished every word when they came their way. When he spoke to them, they felt like they were the only child in Bavaria. They were currently reading *Animal Farm – A Fairy Story* by George Orwell, but they were quickly discovering it had nothing to do with either animals or fairies.

'All power corrupts,' declared Herr Slupski to the class following the opening chapters.

He read books out loud and everyone followed. There were set chapters to read at home to accelerate the story, but few actually read them. Jozef, however, consumed them religiously. He was disappointed when there were no more pages to work through.

The pupils wrote short stories, often about anything they liked and Herr Slupski marked them out of twenty. They were now in their second year at secondary school and Jozef had not yet beat a sixteen. But then only two boys, one of them maddeningly Sebastian, had received a seventeen. Jozef bitterly lamented that fact. He poured his emotions into his pieces, but often languished on fourteens or fifteens.

'Your use of language is to be applauded,' Herr Slupski said to Jozef, who adored the attention but who equally deplored the critique. 'But at times it is incongruous. It does not work. You are forcing words, Jozef.'

Jozef did not listen. He simply continued to look up long words he did not fully understand and shoehorned them into his narratives. He was always hugely impressed with himself – until he saw 'fifteen' scrawled beneath his latest creation in Herr Slupski's unmistakeable hand. Jozef woke early every other Sunday to write his German essays. They were set once a fortnight on Fridays to be handed in on Tuesdays. Jozef always had his done by mid-Sunday morning. Sebastian typically wrote his at the eleventh hour and refused Jozef's exasperated pleas to socialise that night. They did not otherwise spend many evenings apart.

'There are only two chapters left in *Animal Farm*,' Herr Slupski announced at the end of their lesson.

Thin, grey hair was artfully swept over to one side and thick black glasses framed his face. He wore tweed suits and dressed less conventionally than Jozef's other teachers, who were careful to keep their distance. Herr Slupski did not seem to mind. Other teachers seemed desperate to be liked by the pupils, who in turn smelt blood and subsequently preyed on them with ruthless efficiency.

Herr Slupski had begun ruling first by fear and then garnered begrudging respect before earning their unconditional love, which he now returned in spades. However, if anyone dared step out of line he instantly regressed to the furious dictator who had marched up and down the classroom those first few weeks and who had screamed, 'Hitler was a bastard!' one shocking day.

Jozef and, for once, Sebastian were hungry to get home that night and enjoy the end of *Animal Farm*. They had been gripped by the latest pages in class.

It had not snowed again and the constant procession of buses and trams and the odd car had transformed the white blanket over Munich's roads into a mucky brown mess.

The pair of them reached the top of the hill which swooped down to Sebastian's house and they now stood outside the house of the man who had sworn at them so aggressively earlier in the morning.

'You know what I'm going to do?' boasted Jozef, without awaiting a response. 'Get that arse's window!'

Before Sebastian could protest, Jozef's snowball banged against the glass. They careered off like bloodhounds who had been straining at the leash. Sebastian frantically tried to keep pace with his friend and they quickly reached the bottom of the hill, but they were not yet out of sight. The boys were giggling and gasping for breath in the cold, late afternoon, and they were about to congratulate themselves on their courage and sense of justice when Sebastian, a few yards in front of Jozef and turning round to look back, drained white. His eyes flooded with horror. Jozef had no time to react. They were two teenage pups splashing dangerously in the water – and now they had attracted the attention of a large predator hurtling up from the black below. Jozef felt enveloped.

The man had barrelled out of his front door, recalling the two boys from this morning. He launched himself at Jozef, knocking him to the ground.

Jozef felt his winter coat being ripped over his head before the man rained down blows with heavy boots. Numbing shock and a rush of adrenalin spared Jozef from pain. He wasn't sure what was happening or why.

Paralysed, Sebastian was forced to witness the fierce assault on his dear friend.

A woman pushing a pram, with a small child skipping happily alongside, came around the corner of the avenue. The child immediately began to cry.

The man yanked Jozef to his feet, drew his arm back and snapped a shuddering punch to his head. When he spotted the woman, he hastily retreated back up the hill.

Sebastian flicked back to life and supported his friend like a crutch. The two of them were too stunned to speak. The woman wanted to know if Jozef was okay. She lived nearby, but Sebastian, fearing that they had asked for trouble and got it, quickly hauled Jozef away.

'What shall we tell your mother?' he said, panicked.

Jozef still could not think clearly. Blood was trickling down from a cut underneath his left eye. That side of his face felt like a football and his backpack was lassoed around him, chocking his breast. He felt grotesque.

'Frau Diederich!' panicked Sebastian, holding his friend upright at Jozef's door.

CHAPTER THREE

Catharina bathed her boy carefully.

His scarred cheek made Jozef believe he was a monster – until he limped in front of the bathroom mirror and realised it wasn't all that bad. Still, he remained an anxious shell and he hardly touched his supper. Instead, he asked to be excused early from the dining room table and, noticing their son's downcast eyes, his parents immediately acquiesced.

'Of course Jozef,' Catharina agreed gently.

Jozef slowly climbed into bed and was too upset to try and read his latest book. Instead, he faced the wall and choked out an opening sob.

The next morning Sebastian knocked nervously on their door, enquiring if his companion was coming to school but wary to reveal too much.

'No, Sebastian,' said Catharina somewhat sternly. 'Jozef won't be going to school today.'

Jozef heard the exchange from his bedroom upstairs and wanted to rush out after his friend, see his face and at least in that moment begin to confront what had happened. Instead, he stuck to the sanctity of his bed. A breakfast tray remained untouched, bar half a piece of toast soaking in melted butter. Jozef finished a glass of watery orange juice and slipped back to sleep.

He was awoken by a knock at the door downstairs. He did not know what time it was. It was early afternoon and the lady who had witnessed yesterday's disturbing assault had come to see how he was. She knew Catharina by sight, but no more.

'Frau Diederich, I am sorry to trouble you but I wanted to ask how young Jozef is doing. I saw what happened yesterday.'

'Oh, he's fine,' said Catharina. 'Shaken up, that's all. Must have been a nasty fall.'

'Frau Diederich, forgive me. But what exactly did Jozef tell you happened?'

Jozef was horrified when he heard the last question. He had been slowly starting to feel himself again and he was considering getting up, reading his book and hoping to persuade his mother to have an early supper by himself before his father came home. Now he felt sick. His lie to protect his part in inciting yesterday's attack had surely been exposed. Downstairs, words spoken out loud had quietened to careful whispers. Jozef's fragile psyche could hardly take a second volley in as many days. He remained upstairs and briefly considered killing himself.

He imagined who might attend his funeral and who might be most upset. That would teach them, he thought. Of course, he was never really going to do it. He would not be able to enjoy his own funeral were he actually dead.

It was dark when Gerhard finally came up to see him.

Jozef was facing the wall and turned tightly on the far side of the bed. He felt the landing light glare uncomfortably on the back of his head when his father pushed the door ajar.

Catharina had told Gerhard what had happened. Jozef had not fallen in the snow; he had been violently punched and kicked by a man much older and larger than him. Gerhard was struggling to remain calm and avoid marching up the road and tearing to pieces the animal who had attacked his son. But he knew he did not harbour such hostility.

'Jozef, I want to ask you something. Did that man hit you yesterday for throwing a snowball at his window?'

'Yes,' said Jozef, fearing the confession might inflict new wounds on his bruised frame. His diaphragm choked with emotion. He was trying very hard not to break apart completely.

The room fell silent.

The dark had regained control and all Gerhard could see before him was a silhouette of his son cocooned like a caterpillar. Gerhard felt he could say anything in these moments and it would not be repeated too soberly the following day. He wouldn't want it to be. Gerhard loved Jozef very much, but he knew his relationship with him would never eclipse the connection Catharina shared with their son. They chatted away happily about anything and everything over something so mundane as breakfast. Gerhard would perhaps only enjoy such intimacy with Jozef a handful of times in his life. This might be the first of those precious occasions.

'Jozef, I am going to go round to that man's house and I am going to tell him that if he touches you again I will break his legs.'

Jozef loved to hear his father care so much, but that knowledge only made him more emotional and prevented him from rolling over and hugging him. Instead, he gently nodded and murmured where he lay.

Gerhard sensed that would be enough for now and he placed his hand on the back of his shoulder. He squeezed it before slowly releasing his grip and carefully climbing back to his feet. He went downstairs, poured himself a large whisky and drank it impatiently in the hallway like one might gulp coffee before dashing out the door for work in the morning.

'Where are you going?' said Catharina.

'Out,' said Gerhard curtly. The alcohol was working and helping him be cold towards his wife.

'Gerhard, don't go up to that man's house. I don't want you to go. We'll ring the police in the morning. Let them take care of it.'

'The police won't do anything, darling. Why would they?'

'We'll make them, sweetheart. We'll make them,' Catharina pleaded, standing over her husband, who now rose to his feet and prepared to open their front door.

'No,' said Gerhard and he was gone.

Gerhard never revealed what happened the night he went to see the man who beat Jozef.

Catharina never asked and it became something else between them that remained unsaid.

Gerhard unloaded his guilt and grief over the incident that Thursday when Michael visited. Michael smiled and nodded politely when he heard, sipping his whisky with unnatural calm. Inside his blood was raging. He could feel its fury rising. It hadn't deserted him.

'Gerhard, Gerhard. Now, you know to come to me first with these matters, don't you?'

Gerhard nodded like a dog.

Michael looked across the room and saw Jozef was slumped asleep, resting his head against the sofa. He leaned forward, cupping his glass in both hands.

'Gerhard, you have been a good friend, a good Nazi over the years. Now, let me handle this and then we shall never speak of it again. But next time Gerhard...' Michael's voice rose ominously, waking Jozef and forcing

12

him to check the escalation of his threat. 'Next time, Gerhard,' he repeated more calmly. 'You will come to me first and make things easy on yourself and better for Jozef here.'

Michael smiled at the boy.

Jozef, drunk from drowsiness, had no idea what they were talking about. He had long abandoned trying to translate the riddles they often spoke in.

'Yes, yes, of course Michael,' Gerhard said impatiently.

CHAPTER FOUR

Jozef returned to school, sporting a scar which underlined one eye. With distance now between himself and the events of that afternoon, he was even rather proud of it, although everyone bar Sebastian thought he had acquired it by falling over foolishly. Only the two of them appreciated the awful truth.

They had just returned from their lunch hour in the school yard and everyone was drunk on exercise, food and gossip. Jozef and Sebastian sat at the back of class, waiting for the afternoon roll call before heading to double German. Two girls sat giggling nearby. One was Elena Engel, a beautiful, blue-eyed blonde just how Hitler had posterized her on billboards across Germany – bronzed and ready to proudly bear the next generation of National Socialists.

Jozef had had intense feelings for Elena since the first day of secondary school. Her lithe legs were perfect and he was very sweet on her.

Now, egged on by the other girl, she leant across and kissed Jozef's scar. She blushed coyly from the momentary intimacy, but that was nothing compared to Jozef's complexion, which flushed redder than Stalingrad.

Jozef did not care. He was only upset he could not quite experience her kiss, because that side of his face had still not regained full feeling.

'Settle down, settle down. Lunch time is over ladies and gentlemen,' said Herr Slupski at the front of the class.

Jozef and Sebastian, who sat across from one another a few rows from the front, exchanged smiles. They loved it when Herr Slupski called them 'ladies and gentlemen'. Chatter in the room quietened.

'Today,' said Herr Slupski, striding up and down the rows of desks and pupils. 'We are going to deviate slightly from our normal diet of some of the greatest literature ever written and dabble in a spot of modern history.'

Loud sighs.

Jozef and the rest of class had enough of history in history. They didn't need Herr Slupski to give them a second dose – *and* instead of German literature, most pupils' favourite subject.

'Calm down,' Herr Slupski appeased. 'Don't panic. We're not going to delve back very far in the hallowed annals of time. You can think of it more like current affairs, for I am only interested in your friend and mine, Herr Adolf Hitler.'

Excited gasps could be heard around the room.

'And if any of you have any ideas about repeating the fact that we might be getting creative, if you will, with the curriculum this great government has bestowed upon us, I will set the Gestapo on you!' continued Herr Slupski, breaking into a wicked accent.

The pupils laughed, half in humour and half in relief that maybe this wasn't going to be so bad after all.

'Don't think the Gestapo have suddenly disappeared along with Hitler's remains, ladies and gentlemen. They are very much alive and well and thriving along secret channels spreading from right under our noses here in Germany all the way to the furthest reaches of South America. But make no mistake, they are some of the very same people who terrorised entire nations and drove thousands to their deaths in extermination camps.'

Herr Slupski was in full flow. He occasionally paused to sweep what silver hair he had left on his head over to one side – he had just enough to make himself dashing still. Most of the girls in Jozef's class were sweet on him. He had a confident air when he glided down the corridors of their school and a spring in his gait other teachers lacked. They seemed burdened somehow, like life had slowly saddled them with baggage over the years. Herr Slupski did not carry baggage. He carried a tweed jacket, slung casually over his shoulder, which acted peculiarly like a coat hanger. Jozef had not seen anyone carry their jacket like that before.

'How did a far-right fascist party like the National Socialists come to power in one of the most powerful and cultured countries in Europe? How did they go from being a political joke in Germany to moulding our opinions and lives so closely that we tacitly complied with their murderous policy towards Jews and other groups in society that they regarded as enemies of the state or simply superfluous?'

A boy shot his arm up high into the air, straining, reaching, desperate to answer. 'Hitler was superhuman, sir. He was bound to lead,' said the boy, gasping slightly.

'The church says he was the devil and the Nazis' 555ᵗʰ member. The number was an omen, sir,' answered another.

'Fantastic,' exclaimed Herr Slupski, who cherished freethinkers in his class and the boys' egos ballooned until they almost filled the room. 'However, sadly incorrect. But wonderful insight gentlemen. Now let me add some meat to your bones,' he said, waggling his hands and making everyone laugh.

'Hitler was indeed the 555ᵗʰ member of the then new Nazi party – but only officially. In reality, my learned friends, Hitler was only the 55ᵗʰ member of the party. The Nazis started off with 500 fictitious members to make them appear stronger to newcomers. And so they pulled off their first deception aimed at the German public and the world. Therein lie their success and the truth at their heart – the Nazis were never all-powerful like they made out. They were bullies. And what do bullies always do?' Herr Slupski asked, offering the question to the room like a present.

The bullies in class shrank a little in their chairs, while the teacher's favourites, Sebastian included, rose in theirs. Jozef did not move. He did not truly belong in either group. Of course, nobody dared answer the question, which continued to hang uncomfortably in the room. They didn't need to.

'Bullies always act like they are more powerful than they really are. It is a bluff, because that is how bullies flourish. They thrive upon intimidation and fear, and if their bluff is called their power goes up in smoke. Puff,' said Herr Slupski, opening his clenched fist like a flower.

The next morning Jozef and Sebastian bundled into double German, excited about what the lesson may bring and intrigued to know exactly where Herr Slupski was going with their temporary divorce from the school curriculum.

Elena Engel slunk by them both. 'Guten Morgen Jozef,' she purred.

'Oh, hi,' said Jozef, slightly startled as she glided past in a skirt cut teasingly above bronzed knees.

Sebastian gave Jozef a playful push.

'Settle down, settle down,' said Herr Slupski. 'Take your seats, ladies and gentlemen. Then we shall begin. Continuing our little history lesson from the other day, let us explore how the Nazis rose to power in Germany in the 1920s and 1930s, and how Munich, our home, was their birthplace. The Nazis were born out of Germany's surrender and defeat in the Great War in 1918. Two million German troops lay dead in France and the ones who survived – my very self among them – were angry, furious even, at the decision to surrender. There was a strong feeling that politically active men back home, Jews included, were to blame for selling out our soldiers on the front. German soldiers on the Western Front, for example, were still in enemy territory in November 1918. Why had *we* surrendered?'

Herr Slupski had momentarily managed to divert Jozef's mind from thoughts of French kissing Elena Engel like in the movies. He whirled off his jacket and placed it on the back of his chair. Sunlight floated in from the windows. It was a magical morning.

'Textbooks might have you believe the political far left, classically represented by communism and the far right, fascists, lie at opposite ends of the spectrum. Hogwash! The political line is in fact a circle, ladies and gentlemen, and the far left and right lie not at opposite ends of it, but right next to each other. Why?' Herr Slupski asked, pausing. 'Because they are all extremists and they fought for the hearts and minds of German people, people like your parents right here in Munich, Bavaria post-1919.'

That evening, Michael, backed by three associates, knocked on the front door of the man who had assaulted Jozef.

'Guten Abend,' said Michael, bowing to greet him.

'Who are you?'

'We would just like a moment of your time this evening. Might we come inside to talk? More discreetly?'

One of the men behind Michael quickly reached out a hand to block any attempt to close the door.

The man was outflanked. He had a sweetheart, but he lived alone. He let the men in and sat back down in his small, messy front room.

Michael moved a pile of newspapers from the first available chair and sat himself down, uncomfortable for a moment in the disorder, distracted. He was a religiously tidy man, so he composed himself while his three associates came up behind the man. None of them spoke.

'What? What do you want?'

'You have hurt something valuable to me,' said Michael coldly, like a surgeon making an initial incision. 'You attacked and assaulted a boy, Jozef Diederich.'

'That little shit,' the man said.

'Ah,' said Michael, holding an index finger in the air to showcase his point. 'Temper.'

Michael's three associates moved forwards, but Michael shook his head.

The tacit exchange did not go unnoticed by the man, who began to grip his chair more tightly.

'What do you want?' he asked again.

'I want you to leave Jozef Diederich alone and I want you to leave Munich and never return. If you do not, I will find you and we will sit here again. And you do not want to sit here with me again. That would not be wise.' Michael was enjoying himself. It was like the old days.

A dusty timepiece above a scruffy fireplace chimed 9pm. The individuals crowded into the ill-fitting room observed the dongs briefly and the man who had punched Jozef saw his chance and jumped out of his seat. The men were not easily caught out and wrestled him back deep into his moth-eaten spot. The pair flanking him pressed down his arms and sides, while the man behind gripped his head in a chokehold. The man gurgled for air. Michael smiled.

'Are you going to do as I say and leave Munich for good?'

The man struggled in revolt at Michael's question.

Michael held up his hand and the three associates lightened their grip, allowing the man to wheeze uneasily.

'My whole life's in Munich – work, family, my sweetheart. I can't just leave.'

Michael nodded slowly. Experience had taught him what to expect. He nodded his head again, leaving no room for doubt.

His three associates locked in their hold before one of them pulled one of the man's fingers back, the longest, until it snapped out of the joint and was left broken, hanging unnaturally.

The man screamed.

'Will you leave Munich – tonight? My friends will escort you to the train station. I hear there is easy work to be had in Berlin at the moment.'

The man who had punched Jozef nodded gingerly through the shooting pain burning up his arm like bushfire.

'Gut,' said Michael rising from his seat. 'Gentlemen, I will leave our friend in your capable hands. Guten Abend.'

None of them answered.

The man took a train to Berlin that night, like he was told, but he failed to notice Michael's three associates quickly reboard after he was seated. They stole him in a quiet moment when he reached his destination. It was 3am and they hauled him to a back alley behind an old brothel still making ends meet after the war. No one in that district cared to ask why four men were marching through Berlin with such purpose at that time. If they gave it any thought, they assumed one of them was hopelessly drunk and being carried home.

The man who had attacked Jozef did not make it until dawn, discarded unconscious in the alley. Exposure got him before internal bleeding. The brothel's cleaner, a Jew and a survivor of the death camps, found him first thing. He felt nothing, but called the police.

CHAPTER FIVE

'Okay everyone,' said Herr Slupski at the start of the afternoon lessons. 'A bit of order, please. Thank you,' he repeated more warmly when peace had prevailed. 'Okay. Where were we?'

'The Nazis, sir,' said one boy with his hand shooting up high into the air. 'And what helped them come to power in Germany after the Great War.'

'Correct, young man,' replied Herr Slupski, stooping slightly to get into character.

Jozef smiled and instinctively felt Sebastian's gaze – he did not need to glance across to return it.

'The German people, people like your parents, were struggling in 1918, ladies and gentlemen, and they were ripe for a radical party like the National Socialists to persuade them that there was an alternative. The Allied blockade meant Germans were going hungry and thousands were dying of tuberculosis and influenza. Herr Hitler could play on all of those factors. In 1917 Russia, one of the Allied powers fighting against Germany, pulled out of the First World War in disarray after a Communist revolution brought Lenin to power. Munich itself followed suit.'

Small gasps and quizzical faces were shared between pupils. Most of them had not heard of this.

Herr Slupski half smiled and glanced up momentarily.

More than twenty sets of hungry eyes were trained on him like snipers.

'That's right, ladies and gentlemen. Munich became a mini communist republic for a little over two months in early 1919 until right-wing government troops were ordered to crush it.'

A blackbird suddenly crashed into a window near Sebastian. He jumped, startled.

'It's okay, young Sebastian,' said Herr Slupski, seizing on the moment and racing to Jozef's friend's side. 'Maybe it's the communists,' he teased, turning Sebastian bright red while the rest of class laughed. He winked kindly at Sebastian before continuing.

'The leaders of the Munich communist republic were mainly Jewish and, in average German eyes, 1919 inextricably linked the two together. This was 'evidence',' Herr Slupski underlined his words by miming inverted commas with long fingers.

Jozef paid less attention than normal in German that afternoon. He had a football match, the biggest of the school year so far, straight after the final bell. It was at home, so at least they didn't have to travel, but it was a cup semi-final against one of the largest schools in Munich. The more boys a school had, a simple law of averages meant that they had more and better footballers to form an XI from. Their opponents that afternoon certainly had some good players, some of the very best in Munich in Jozef's age group. Jozef knew only too well. He played alongside most of them every Sunday in Munich's boys' football league.

Jozef played for the best side in the city, but he was the only one from his school who did so. His schoolmates played for less fashionable teams on the weekend, if they played at all, preferring instead to experiment with beer and nicotine and girls.

He would be man-marking the opposition's star playmaker in central midfield, Jürgen Fiedler, who was bigger than Jozef, but who was not as quick or skilful. But Jürgen Fiedler had a 'name' in boys' football in Munich and had long been on the radar of professional clubs in the city, who cherry-picked the best boys and offered them two-year apprenticeships when they reached the age of 16.

Despite his ability, Jozef was largely a forgotten face when it came to Munich's pecking order to win a professional football apprenticeship. He secretly resented his father for not being pushier and making sure he didn't lose what position he thought he had in that queue. Jozef was becoming quietly convinced that not having a parent who turned up pitchside on Sunday mornings looking flash and middle-class and constantly talking up their son's talent was allowing other boys to unfairly jump ahead.

Still, Jozef could have his revenge on the Jürgen Fiedlers of this world while representing his school. He could scrap, kick and claw his way to victory and there was nothing any parent on the sidelines could do about it. He was used to being berated by the parents of the boys he played with on the weekend, and told to 'calm down' and 'take it easy'. Such jeers only spurred Jozef on. Playing the underdog was in his blood.

Gerhard knew how much Jozef's big match meant to him. He knew his son would raise his game today, because he could see how desperate he was to win for his school on such occasions. He was never more proud of Jozef, but he could not bring himself to say so. Gerhard had thought of telling him through Catharina. She could get the message across. But then she didn't understand football, so Gerhard wrongly believed that she did not understand her son on days like these. Instead, Gerhard admired from afar.

In last year's Munich Boys' Schools Cup, Jozef's team against the odds reached the final where no one gave them a prayer against the most powerful and fashionable school in Munich. Jozef had the game of his young life and helped inspire his school to a dramatic 4-1 upset. The other parents from Jozef's Sunday side had barracked Jozef heavily from the stands all game. Jozef, for once, could not hear them and proceeded to kick the opposition's prize player to pieces. The more he complained, the harder Jozef kicked because for once Jozef was outpaced. It hardly ever happened, but Jozef's opponent that day could run like the wind.

That successful individual battle laid the foundations for his teammates to push forward and prevail. With his winners' medal proudly clenched in his fist, Jozef looked up to the stands to spot his father while trooping triumphantly down the players' tunnel. He felt like a star. He spotted Gerhard, sat with parents from his Sunday side. Father and son raised their fists in jubilation and both secretly treasured the exchange.

Gerhard was late and missed today's first half. Work had delayed him, which made him furious. Now he was here and soon heard it was 2-2. Jozef's school had twice rebounded from falling behind. They were giving as good as they got. Michael timed himself beautifully to see every kick.

Jozef had spotted him but disappointingly not his father, but he couldn't think about them now. He had to concentrate. 2-2 became 3-3 after half-time. Again Jozef's school had equalised in what had quickly escalated into a war of attrition. Whose will would break first?

Jozef lay on the ground after one heated challenge in the engine room of the contest. It was muddy and he was suddenly exposed, prostrate on the turf. Jürgen Fiedler saw his opportunity and ran past, kicking Jozef while the referee wasn't looking. The blow stung the back of his calf.

Michael saw it. He wasn't mad. Boys will be boys, he thought. He wanted to see how Jozef reacted; he wanted to see what he was really made of. Michael didn't care for 'good Nazis'. Millions were 'good Nazis' during the war. Michael wanted great ones.

Jozef's school was starting to get on top and threatening to take the lead for the first time in the match, but now Jürgen Fiedler was counter-attacking at pace down the wing and Jozef was one of only two defenders, outnumbered, tracking back. He could not allow Jürgen to beat him and pass to a supporting teammate. 4-3 would be a bridge too far for Jozef's school at this heady juncture. Jürgen took a heavy touch and Jozef had his chance just past the halfway line. The two opponents were on collision course. Jozef sneered. He did not know why but he hated Jürgen Fiedler and everything his privilege represented, and he felt that distaste rushing to the surface now. He slammed into his opponent, tossing the boy onto the ground and ballooning the ball harmlessly out of play.

'Scheisse!' cried Jürgen, lying muddied at the feet of spectating parents.

'Come on, Jozef!' cried a parent in protest.

Jozef was still sneering and said nothing before trotting away to restart play.

'Great tackle, Jozef! Well played,' cheered Michael, applauding loudly. No one told him to be quiet.

The next morning Jozef still had yesterday's epic match in his stiff legs. It was the talk of the school.

'Brilliant match!' Herr Slupski commented in Jozef's ear while everyone settled down for double German. 'You were fantastic – quite fantastic.'

Jozef smiled. This was personal praise from the most popular teacher in school, but his tired mind weighed heavy and he currently could not muster anything more positive.

Herr Slupski was disappointed even that he had not elicited a more excited response from his pupil.

'You've got sexy legs,' said Elena Engel, hurrying past Jozef while clasping school books close to her bosom.

'Thanks,' replied Jozef, his face flushing at the compliment from the focus of his rapidly exploding emotions.

Jozef had developed cramp in the later stages of yesterday's match and, in front of a crowd of classmates and pupils from his school, had had to receive treatment on the pitch, stretching tightened calves high up in the air, so that they were revealed to all, including girls secretly sweet on him.

Herr Slupski felt charged today and launched himself straight into the lesson. 'By 1921 Adolf Hitler was the leader of the then German Workers' Party, soon renamed the National Socialist German Workers' Party or

Nazis for short. His rhetoric was simple and relentless,' he began, taking off his jacket and placing it on the back of his chair.

'He spoke about the injustice of the Treaty of Versailles, Germany's terms of surrender after the First World War. Paying reparations to France crippled Germany's economy. Inflation smashed through the roof. People were demoralised, utterly. Hitler was not alone in making public such views. There were lots of right-wing parties springing up in Bavaria at the time and their message was the same – Versailles was a crime and Jews were behind it.'

Jozef enjoyed a rush of adrenalin as he caught sight of Elena Engel's exposed leg. She was not wearing socks above her brown shoes and Jozef thought he might burst. His face flushed hot before he forced it back down and his normal colour returned.

'Hitler's sheer energy and zeal set him apart from rival right-wing parties. That dynamism attracted other political talent, which helped elevate the Nazis to a position of unrivalled power in Germany by 1933. Hermann Goering, who became Hitler's deputy, said, 'I joined because they were revolutionaries, not because of any ideological nonsense'.'

Herr Slupski put on a wicked German accent for his impersonation of Goering and reached out toward the pupils closest to him. Everyone laughed.

'On November 8, 1923,' he continued, 'Hitler called for a national revolution right here in Munich, Bavaria. The next day the Nazis and other right-wing parties marched through the city, but the government ordered police to crush the protest and 16 Nazis were killed in the crossfire. Four policemen died. Hitler fled.'

This didn't sound like the Hitler the world knew and feared, Jozef thought, imagining a selfish Führer scuttling away to save himself.

'Hitler was tried in court for the part he played in those deaths in early 1924. It was a media sensation. Entrance to the public gallery, typically empty for everyday cases, was by ticket only. Hitler spoke powerfully and eloquently to the packed courtroom,' said Herr Slupski, unfolding his arms theatrically.

'He defended himself and boldly told the presiding judge, 'History will be my judge'. Brave? Foolish? Neither,' Herr Slupski responded in answer to his own question. 'It was a con. Hitler knew the judge. Unbeknownst to almost everyone in court that day, Hitler had stood before the same judge two years earlier in 1922 for his part in violently disrupting a left-wing political meeting. The judge was sympathetic to Hitler that day and he was sympathetic to him again in 1924 – Hitler served a short prison sentence. He was now a hero and, more dangerously, a martyr.'

A sense of injustice started to fill the room like water. Jozef turned and made eye contact with Sebastian.

'In the mid-1920s Germany's economy recovered, inflation fell and the good times were back – but only temporarily. American dollars were footing the bill, not German marks. The day would come when Washington would call in those loans and economic gloom would return, playing right into Hitler's hands.'

CHAPTER SIX

'People were calling for a simple life in the 1920s,' said Michael, sipping Gerhard's best whisky in the Diederich's living room. 'They wanted to enjoy the outdoors. They did not want decadence. Jewry was wasteful and flaunted its wealth. I know you felt the same Gerhard,' Michael continued, inviting his host to join in the right-wing rhetoric. 'Hitler was clever back then. He used that movement to recruit the Hitler Youth.'

'Yes, yes,' said Gerhard hurriedly, brushing over the invitation and pouring himself another drink.

Their living room felt tired tonight. Catharina had not cleaned up fully from their dinner party the other evening with the Gottliebs, and Gerhard sensed Michael's disapproval.

'Why did you join the brown shirts Michael?' he said.

'Jewry wanted to rule the world. We could not let that happen. I gladly joined. There was nowhere else for me to channel my feelings towards the left. And my family disapproved violently, so I knew it must be right,' he smiled.

Gerhard himself had supported Hitler fervently in the 1930s. Even Catharina had done so, but his wife had her doubts when war seemed inevitable and Gerhard privately turned on Hitler in 1942 following the invasion of Russia. Gerhard had known Hitler was deranged then and had only ever wanted to blow the whole world to oblivion, and everyone back home in Germany with it.

'But Hitler was insane,' said Gerhard, cradling his drink and interrupting his own train of thought.

'Hitler was not insane, he was just,' replied Michael, searching for the right words. 'Just emotional Gerhard – impatient, stubborn and disorganised.' He smiled again. It was rare for him to be this drunk and it was making him sentimental.

'Hitler was often late for meetings. He hated them,' Michael reminisced. 'He believed in Darwin. I had that in common with him – the survival of the fittest. We survived Gerhard. Jozef survived. You don't know how important he is to us do you?'

The clock struck 10pm. Catharina would be home soon. Michael was normally comfortably gone by this hour, ensuring he and Catharina remained vessels in the black, knowing the other was out there somewhere but preferring not to see.

'Jozef's mother and father are still alive,' said Michael.

Gerhard lost grip of one arm of his chair and instinctively grabbed the other, clinging to it grimly. He felt he was aboard a ship which had been catastrophically torpedoed. He could see Michael was talking because his mouth was moving but he could not hear the words.

Gerhard had always believed Jozef's parents died in the war. He also knew Jozef was special to Michael, but no more. Jozef was just a boy, in need of loving parents. Gerhard and Catharina had met that natural need. His senses began to swim back to the surface.

'Gerhard,' Michael said. 'Gerhard.'

Gerhard looked up and caught Michael's eyes.

Michael felt sympathy for him but only the sympathy one felt for a dog.

'You have always known what you needed to know,' he said. 'You needed to know Jozef's birth parents were dead and now you need to know that they are very much alive. You needn't worry about his mother. She is still in Munich.'

'Oh God!' exclaimed Gerhard.

'She is still in Munich,' Michael repeated. 'But she has lost faith. She does not believe anymore. We would rather kill Jozef with our own hands than allow her near him – and we would never hurt a hair on that boy's head. As I said, he is too important.'

'Where is Jozef's father?' said Gerhard, still unseated in his panic.

'Safe. He is no longer with the mother.'

'Who is he?' asked Gerhard and as soon as the words fell from his lips he did not know if he meant Jozef or his biological father.

'That is something you do not need to know. Catharina must also never know. She is... she is unstable. This you know.'

Gerhard looked up and saw Catharina standing in the doorway.

'Darling,' said Gerhard. 'We didn't hear you come in.'

Fear filled her husband's eyes, which blinked out among the drab upholstery like beacons.

'Catharina,' said Michael, rising to his feet and kissing her on the cheek. 'You look beautiful. I am afraid I have led your husband astray this evening. We have drunk rather too much. Now I must go. Gerhard – it has been wonderful. Remember what we talked about.'

'Yes. Yes.'

The second word sounded more like an apology.

'What were you talking about?' enquired Catharina after Michael had left. She had her wits about her and it was clear her husband did not fully have his.

'What? Sorry, darling?'

'What were you talking about?' she repeated more accusingly.

'Nothing,' he said weakly.

CHAPTER SEVEN

Elena Engel allowed Jozef to gently stroke her leg during lunchtime. Her perfectly soft skin made the finest silk seem unhewn.

She liked it, Jozef thought, sat happily in the warm sunshine on the school playing field. He was going out of his mind and was in heaven for the thrilling few heartbeats.

'Would you like to meet up this weekend?' she said, switching her gaze to Jozef's kind face.

'This weekend? Right. Yes, of course,' Jozef stuttered, unsure of what he had done to deserve such a wild upturn in fortune in his previously non-existent love life. Polite boys did badly when it came to girls, Jozef had convinced himself. 'What do you want to do?' he asked.

'Call round for me on Saturday after supper and we can go for a walk,' she replied, confidently rising to her feet and breaking off Jozef's touch.

Jozef watched her transfixed as she left him alone on the worn grass baked yellow by the hot season. He collected himself but did not feel his feet touch the ground as he followed her to his first lesson of the afternoon, double German.

'Guten Nachmittag ladies and gentlemen,' said Herr Slupski.

No reply.

'Guten Nachmittag ladies and gentlemen,' he repeated, louder this time.

'Guten Nachmittag sir,' the class repeated in unison.

'Danke,' said Herr Slupski, returning to a more jovial state. 'Just checking you were all still breathing.'

Collective giggles put everyone at ease.

'In 1928, the Nazis received 2.6 per cent of the vote in the general election. Less than five years later in 1933, Adolf Hitler was chancellor and the most powerful man in Germany. How did he do it?' Herr Slupski asked, rolling up his white sleeves tightly above his elbows.

'Well,' he continued, opening a large top window with a long pole commandeered from behind the blackboard. 'I'm going to tell you.' A soothing breeze from the field instantly cooled the space.

Jozef caught sight of Elena Engel over his shoulder. She smiled at him. Sebastian did not miss their moment and was concerned.

'In 1929 the Wall Street crash in the United States of America triggered the Great Depression. Germany was hardest hit of all the developed nations. Unemployment shot up; food became prohibitively expensive; people were miserable. Germany's five major banks were all bankrupt by 1931. Twenty thousand businesses in Germany, businesses your parents owned and tirelessly ran, were also bankrupt. The German middle classes were badly hit.'

Herr Slupski took a sip of water.

'The Nazis' message had not changed magically during all that time. Hitler still insisted Germany needed to be reborn and that Jews were to blame. But now, ladies and gentlemen, your parents were ready to listen. 37 per cent of Germans, more than one in three, voted for Hitler in the elections in July 1932, giving him the largest share of the vote.'

'No one could tell if National Socialism was something good with bad side effects or something bad with good side effects. What people did not know was that the Nazis were very nearly bankrupt at this time as well. Hitler, Goering et al. could have been blown away in the wind, ladies and gentlemen. So what saved them from the brink? Humanity. In January 1933 politicians bowed to popular pressure and Hitler was offered the chancellorship as part of a coalition government. They foolishly thought that they could tame Hitler and control him better from within the Reichstag than outside it. They were wrong.'

Jozef lied and told his parents he was visiting Sebastian's house that Saturday night. Sebastian was devastated. He couldn't recall the last Saturday evening he had spent apart from his friend. Jozef had agonised all afternoon over what to wear. Those hours now turned out to be largely wasted when he opened his wardrobe. Everything felt unfashionable. Everything felt old.

Elena Engel had had the same problem, although Jozef would never have believed it. She was effortlessly elegant in his love-struck eyes. She lived with her mother and stepfather above the family shop.

It was dark and uninviting now and 7.30pm precisely.

Jozef was a stickler for punctuality. He could not help it. He had given himself very nearly half an hour to complete the five-minute walk from his home to Elena's and he had had to endure endless laps of the streets near where they lived to take him up to 7.30pm precisely. He felt he had relived the moment ten times over by the time he tentatively knocked on the Engels' door. He heard someone bound loudly down stairs. Elena. She was wearing a red silk dressing gown, a gift from her mother last Christmas. She was not ready. She too had been 'not ready' for close to half an hour, waiting impatiently for Jozef to knock and 'catch' her getting dressed.

'What has gotten into you this evening?' her mother had complained.

'Nothing,' she had lied calmly.

'Hi Jozef,' she now said casually.

Jozef, already drunk on excitement, almost blew his top when he saw Elena half-dressed before him. Her dressing gown was tied tightly at its top, but blew liberally open around her legs, which must have been the most stunning in Munich.

'I'll just be a minute,' Elena said. On cue and as rehearsed all week in front of her bedroom mirror, she flicked out a bare leg before swishing back seductively upstairs to dress.

Jozef couldn't breathe.

A few hours later she became the first girl he French kissed. It was a bit wet, if the truth be told, and almost like a race – who could open and close their mouth the fastest while waggling their tongue wildly around?

Jozef was quite happy for Elena to win on that count. He was too busy getting to grips with her bottom at the time.

Those few hours walking the streets of Munich, running and talking and grabbing and French kissing, were the happiest of Jozef's life so far. He did not feel the cold; he did not feel the ground beneath his feet. He felt happy.

One week and three dates later he was heartbroken. Elena had abandoned him for an older, more experienced boy. Humiliatingly, the whole school knew.

'Dumped by Elena Engel after one week,' goaded one greasy classmate.

Jozef did not flinch. He was a veteran of hiding his true feelings. Still, something in Jozef changed that summer. He learnt to only trust himself. Who else could he rely upon? His mother? His father? Michael? Sebastian? His instincts told him perhaps the least likely of those candidates – Michael.

31

CHAPTER EIGHT

Jozef wiped the steam from his inadequate mirror and saw his reflection staring blankly back. This won't do, he complained bitterly in his head. Still, it was his mirror; it was his room; it was his new home. It was 1959 and Jozef felt different. His teenage years had been largely kind. He had remained athletically slim, he had escaped the worst scars acne could inflict and his boyish good looks were accompanying him happily into adulthood.

He moved away from the corner of the cramped room in the undergraduate halls at Berlin university and sat on his bed and cried – really cried for the first time since he was very small. The initial tears escalated and finally graduated to heaving, breathless sobs which lifted his whole frame like some medieval torture. He was drowning. He could not breathe. Emotion seemed to be eating him alive from inside out. Breathe, he tried to tell himself.

Jozef's parents had left him a few lifetimes earlier and now all he could see were four years reaching out before him forever. Four life sentences. What had he done? How stupid had he been? Jozef had arrived at the end of day one, week one, year one of a four-year degree in modern history at the University of Berlin. He had been so desperate to leave the home he had grown to hate in Munich behind. Now, all he wanted to do was board the first train back. Drunken giggles could be heard outside. Jozef's fellow first years had wasted little time finding new companions, companions they were now escorting to the undergraduates' union to get wildly intoxicated with and melt the ice of social discomfort they all currently felt. Jozef would rather have gone to the gas chamber.

All he had was four grim walls – his home for the next academic year at least. There was a single bed, a large beaten wardrobe, which badly needed cleaning, and a simple sink headlined by a small mirror, which had its own light chain. You pulled it and highlighted in stunning detail every blemish and tiny imperfection on your face. It wasn't having the desired effect on Jozef's fragile confidence.

Bang, bang, bang.

Jozef jumped out of his skin. He froze, praying the noise would go quietly.

'Hello? Hello?' sounded an alien voice on the other side of Jozef's thick wooden door.

He flicked to autopilot and opened it without replying.

'Hello dear fellow. My name is Mathias. I am living just across the hall. Would you like to come out for a few beverages this evening?'

More drunken giggles from desperate hangers-on. Mathias was drunk and holding a half-empty bottle of red wine in one hand. He was wearing a black leather trenchcoat, not unlike a Nazi and he was flanked by two other boys. A fourth, with long hair, was collapsed worryingly on the floor behind them, drunk beyond measure and struggling to remain conscious.

'Well dear fellow?' said Mathias.

'Oh, sorry,' said Jozef.

'Would you like to come and get very drunk not unlike a skunk?' said Mathias.

'Err... no,' said Jozef.

Mathias was stunned.

'Err, no, sorry. I have a prior engagement with friends in town,' Jozef continued, lying to protect his pride.

'Suit yourself,' Mathias sniffed, a little hurt. 'Good night.'

The three boys lurched arm in arm down the narrow corridor and were quickly followed by the boy bedraggled on the ground, hauling himself to his feet. He momentarily smiled at Jozef.

Jozef returned the compliment and fleetingly felt he might have an ally. He closed the door to his room again and breathed deeply. The verbal exchange had at least temporarily wrenched him out of his depression. He would go for some air and a walk around campus. He could get his bearings and then go to bed and sleep. Tomorrow was another day. It couldn't get any worse than the last two.

The night before Jozef left home for university his mother and father had sat him down.

'Jozef, you are adopted,' his father had said flatly.

His greying mother, Catharina, had sat there dutifully observing rank behind her husband.

Jozef's head had swayed like a boxer who had been hit.

Catharina had ached to grab hold of her son, her baby, but Gerhard's presence and temper prevented her. It was one more thing she never forgave him for.

'You're not my parents,' Jozef had finally said, mimicking his father's monotone.

'We believe we are your parents,' Gerhard had replied. 'But now we believe the time is right that you know that, no, we are not your birth parents.'

Eighteen years of things unsaid collapsed in seconds. How easily. The honesty in the room had been beyond disturbing. Who were these strangers sat opposite him, Jozef had suddenly thought. 'Are my real parents alive?' he had asked.

Catharina's heart ached at the word 'real'.

Gerhard had been expecting the question. 'No,' he had said firmly. 'Your mother died in a bombing raid here in Munich during the war and your father was captured by the Russians in Stalingrad. He was sent to Siberia after the war and died in a prisoner-of-war camp in 1951.'

Jozef's head had swum again. First, he had learned he was adopted and the two people he had shared the vast majority of his young life with had been revealed to be relative imposters. Now, he had learned his true mother and father were dead. At that point he had started to really worry about university. He had been so excited about going for so long that the emotion had almost exhausted itself. But his nerves were unsettling him now deeply.

He stood outside in the dark. Drunken cries and music from the undergraduates' union rumbled in the distance like artillery on the Western Front. It felt like it was coming from another world. He breathed in the October air and stretched his legs around surroundings still alien to him. University campus was cocooned close but away from the hustle of real life and central Berlin.

The intimidating size of its buildings leaned over him, suffocating him again. He tried to catch his breath, forming ghosts out of fog in front of his face. He walked quickly to escape the sensation and lost track of time. He could see an expensive car filing past a few hundred yards below. Jozef did not want to venture further. At least he felt a perverse sense of safety here.

He was displaced physically for the first time in his life as well as displaced emotionally. He did not know where home was – or where it had ever been. He thought buried and long locked away in his memory was the image of his true parents, who had created him and tended to him gently as a newborn. It felt strange knowing that what he wanted to know above everything was buried within him.

Drunken cries were edging closer. Jozef saw a group of stragglers merrily swaying up the hill from the direction of the city and the outside world – three of them, arm in arm like sailors on leave. They were singing, but Jozef couldn't make out what. He quickly crossed the road to avoid any possible confrontation. The scars from the day the man had beaten him for throwing a snowball at his window had faded, forgotten on his skin, but psychologically they resurfaced in panics like this. Jozef broke out in a sweat before the party marched happily, harmlessly past. They hadn't even noticed him.

Jozef's confidence had taken a pounding in the last two years. His friendship with Sebastian was not the same. They had effectively been divorced and had only just got back together. Sebastian had met a girl, who had never liked Jozef. She viewed him as competition and had cruelly eliminated him from her new sweetheart's life. Jozef didn't care for her, but he cared deeply for Sebastian, who had betrayed that emotion he felt.

The girl had dropped Sebastian abruptly at the start of the summer. Jozef, still desperate to get back with his friend, scarcely dare believe it, but Sebastian hadn't taken the hint. It was not over in his naïve eyes until a few weeks later when, distraught, Sebastian had raced out of a pub in town. Jozef had been with him and known then.

Jozef, who all the girls at school had been sweet on, ironically remained a virgin. His week-long romance with Elena Engel was all he really had to show for his good looks and as a result he was still innocent when it came to the opposite sex. Sebastian had had intercourse during his one relationship like it had been going out of style, which pained Jozef. He felt left behind by the one peer he thought he could trust. Then Sebastian had gone to university in Frankfurt to study science.

The first week of university in Berlin was a dizzying round of fairs and enrolments. Which clubs to join; which societies; who to associate with? Jozef could not decide. He just wanted classes to begin and some structure to his day – and he wanted something to take his mind off this debilitating homesickness, which made him cry most evenings and which undermined what little confidence he had. That first week crawled by like a month. Jozef did not befriend anyone, never really talked. If he did, he almost immediately disliked people, who were overly confident and aggressively arrogant. He was beginning to wonder if everyone at university was like that.

Jozef had feared this. He had billed this great adventure as 'the first in his family to go to university'. His father, Gerhard, was a skilled working-class man and now Jozef was going to enter the professions and lower middle-classes or climb even higher. But that sounded like nonsense now. He did not know his true circumstances. Maybe he was the family dreamer – the one who foolishly tried to become a professional footballer, the one who underachieved. Jozef knew that he perhaps could have achieved more so far in his life, but he had done his best. So many things now clouded his past.

CHAPTER NINE

For the first time since arriving in Berlin, Jozef had a spring in his step. It was Monday morning, the first day of class. Thank Christ, he thought before apologising to the heavens with a smile for blaspheming. Week one was behind him and like a bad dream. The sun was shining despite a bite in the air and the sky was blue and clean like his mood. He could see the sun rising and warming the bottom corner of the world from his window – he was no longer a prisoner looking out his grey cell. Life wasn't so bad after all, he thought.

It was breathtakingly cold in halls in the morning. The building's pipes took time to crank up ill-temperedly after being turned off for the night. Jozef saw the charm in it for the first time as he pulled up his trousers around his shrinking waist. Temporary depression had killed his appetite and he had lost weight.

He checked his features quickly in the mirror and swept his mousy hair, dishevelled from sleep, over to one side. He suddenly remembered how handsome he was as he prepared to scrub his face in his tiny sink. Jozef had few blemishes. He had slept for Germany this last week, had not drunk and was a picture of health compared to most undergraduates. He peered deeper into his green eyes. He felt like himself again.

'I can do this,' he said out loud.

He turned the cold tap on – there was no hot – and freezing water spluttered out, quickly filling the basin, which could only take a couple of pints of liquid. Jozef, who had blossomed into a 6ft-tall young man, had to stoop awkwardly to splash water onto his face. If he was not careful he cracked his head sharply on the protruding tap when he rose back up and cursed loudly. If his immediate neighbours in university halls were in, they were startled. They did not think this painfully quiet individual hid such fury.

Jozef washed his face with soap and rinsed it clean with running water. He did not like to use the water he had just muddied with dirty skin. He felt he was undoing his good work. Jozef was particular that way. He had an ordered mind and he liked to tick things off in his head when they were done. It made him feel good; he knew where he was, he knew what he had achieved and what still needed to be tackled. Now, he had an utterly unsettling chasm to fill in his personal history – who am I?

He enjoyed the walk from his room in the tower block at the top of campus, winding his way downstream through the early morning rush. This was new for everyone and Jozef revelled in the fact that they were all now in the same uncomfortable boat. There were people like him, pacing alone; there were people who had wet hair who, unlike Jozef, had preferred every precious moment in bed to preparing quietly and conscientiously for the academic day ahead; and there were people who looked a mess and who were clearly still intoxicated from one last night of revelry. Their influence and patter were beginning to grate, Jozef sensed. Thank God, he thought again and his mood improved some more.

Eventually Jozef reached the bottom of another large tower block, which served as the main lecture hall and the home of the majority of academic departments, including modern history. He climbed flights of stairs until he reached floor seven. He already knew exactly where he was supposed to be, because he had done a dry run of this morning's commute the previous week. Jozef's mind had demanded he do it, otherwise he would not have been able to sleep, panicked by uncertainty. Now he walked down a narrow corridor until he reached Professor Zielinski's door, fifth on the left, first past the secretary's office. Five-to-nine. Perfect.

'Come in young man,' greeted the professor, wearing a deep green suit and matching bow tie. His hair was an unkempt mop of greying curls and he was exactly how Jozef had imagined him back home in Munich over the summer.

He was the first to arrive.

'In good time,' said the professor cheerily. 'A man after my own heart.'

Jozef smiled. It was the first pleasant thing anyone had said to him all week.

'And who might you be young man?' asked the professor, sat across from Jozef in the small box room, which was no bigger than Jozef's childhood bedroom. Impossibly crowded shelves of books, a lifetime of learning, leaned up on all sides of the space.

'Jozef,' he answered nervously. 'Jozef Diederich.'

'Herr Diederich. Ah, yes,' said the professor, looking down his list of undergraduates. 'You are one of six I am expecting this morning.'

The last to arrive was a young lady who had failed her first year at university and who was now resitting it. She was a relatively seasoned student and apologised 'profusely' for the late intrusion before making a maddening commotion with her bag and belongings.

Professor Zielinski knew she did not mean a word of it. Frau Kluge was always late. The professor had wanted to throw her out of the department but had been outvoted by his fellow history professors who quietly fantasised about her.

Frau Kluge spoke a lot but made little sense, a trait Professor Zielinski deplored. He preferred quiet contemplation and then only concise utterances rather than Frau Kluge's 100-words-a-minute bluster before revealing anything of real note. Frau Kluge dominated the early debate – Professor Zielinski had feared as much. His class of shy first-years didn't stand a chance. Frau Kluge wore dark glasses, which she lied were for an eye condition but which really hid a hard night drinking. An avalanche of them had buried any ambition of passing her first year exams. Professor Zielinski, wearied by Frau Kluge's aggressive but misinformed arguments, drew the debate to an early close.

'Seeing as we haven't heard most of you speak this morning, which is slightly disappointing, might I ask a question? What, do you suppose, is the worst thing that could happen this year?'

'You fail,' said Frau Kluge as soon as the words left Professor Zielinski's mouth.

'No, Frau Kluge,' said the professor with a sigh. 'Anyone else?'

Jozef felt he knew the answer. This knowledge made him flush with excitement but also with embarrassment. He had felt horribly outgunned in IQ terms in the first university seminar of his academic life. How could he know anything everyone else did not? Blank faces around the room. Someone else piped up. Blast, thought Jozef. They had beaten him to it. He should have been braver.

'We start World War III,' said another boy.

'Well, that would be pretty bad,' said the professor, more agreeably. 'But perhaps not quite.'

'We die,' said Jozef, simply and without invitation.

Professor Zielinski smiled and looked at him. He had been hoping he would speak for the last half an hour. 'Thank you, Herr Diederich. Finally, someone with perspective. Dismissed.'

Everyone bundled out of the room, bags wrapped around themselves and preventing Jozef from climbing out of his seat until only he and the professor remained.

'You too Herr Diederich,' said the professor, smiling and without looking up.

CHAPTER TEN

Gerhard and Catharina sat down for dinner. Catharina had prepared it promptly because she knew tonight was Michael's evening for coming round to drink with her husband.

Gerhard, famished after hardly eating all day, would normally ask for hearty portions when he arrived home. Not tonight. 'That is fine darling,' he said when she had served only a modest plate.

Catharina knew why. Her husband did not like to drink on a full stomach. It, one, stopped him becoming drunk quite so quickly and, two, alcohol only then further bloated him, he informed her. Catharina no longer went singing in the Munich ladies' choir on Thursday evenings. Some of the other women had become dismissive of her and she had had enough and resigned, though fearing she was perhaps giving them what they wanted.

'There will come a day when none of us can entertain their kind in this world,' said Frau Richter-Ostermann, the chairwoman of the choir's board.

Catharina had not been supposed to hear that observation upon entering the ladies' restroom during a break in the rehearsal.

Frau Richter-Ostermann had been unrepentant. 'No need, ladies,' she said when her coven flinched and prepared to skulk away upon Catharina's entrance. 'We are done here.'

The sad truth was Catharina would have agreed with her colleagues had they cared to ask. Catharina now went to bed early on Thursday evenings with her latest book. She made herself a hot water bottle and a mug of hot chocolate and read for two, sometimes three, hours before finally feeling sleepy and turning in for the night. She had come to cherish these occasions. They gave her time to herself, time away from her husband – time she needed. She had all day, every day to herself now Jozef was in Berlin, but that still was not enough. When Gerhard returned home from work it felt like an intrusion. What are you doing back so early, she would snap in her head.

Their home had seemed so cramped, so chaotic while Jozef was growing up and they had had Sebastian round every other evening. She had pined for extra space during those happy years. Now her house felt like an aircraft hangar. She could have invited the Red Army round for supper and still had room to spare if Gerhard decided to drink in the other room. Their home had been emptied of Jozef's belongings and energy.

Gerhard was just a man she lived with, someone she shared a bed with. They were no longer intimate. The only married thing she did in that regard was offer a cheek to be pecked routinely before Gerhard left for work every morning. That was it. Catharina had long stopped feeling those kisses. It was like brushing up to an inanimate object – nothing.

'How was your day, darling?' Gerhard asked while they ate.

At least he was chirpy. He was about to get drunk and had been looking forward to the sensation all day.

Catharina felt her husband had started communicating in another language. She did not understand him and had no idea what to utter in reply. 'Fine,' she said.

'Did you speak to anyone nice?' said Gerhard, fast exhausting the short stock list of questions he repeated for his wife every evening.

'No one,' answered Catharina blankly. She sipped the last of the modest glass of wine she had enjoyed while preparing tonight's meal. She had finished her plate and she could see her husband had done so and was now reading his newspaper, *Süddeutsche Zeitung*, while his food settled for a moment. Then he would be up and pouring himself drinks in preparation for Michael. Even though the room and their home felt vast now, the square dinner table they shared appeared tiny. Gerhard was uncomfortably close to her, despite having his head firmly in today's headlines.

'How is Jozef settling in at university?' Michael asked Gerhard later that evening, whisky in one hand and the other resting comfortably on the arm of the Diederich's best chair.

'Fine, fine,' said Gerhard.

'Any homesickness? It's a big step.'

'No, I don't think so,' said Gerhard, quietly inebriated and unwittingly repeating the lie Jozef had told him on the telephone a few days earlier. 'Jozef said he was surprised himself he had not felt more homesick.'

'Gut,' said Michael, happy that Gerhard did not now know his previously gregarious son had become a loner and cried alone in his room at night while fellow undergraduates went out drinking and socialising.

Michael had placed a spy close to Jozef, reporting back on his early movements away from home. He knew Mathias' father and had made sure Mathias went to the same institution as Jozef. It had not proved difficult. The Nazis' true triumph was their unfeeling efficiency and ability to transform previously God-fearing innocents into quiet monsters. Mathias' father was a Catholic priest and had been one of the few in the influential church to sympathize with the Nazis during their twelve years in power. The church was the only institution to stand up to Hitler with any real success at home and live to tell the tale.

The Nazis did not solely target Jews and communists. They targeted anyone who physically and mentally strayed from their pure Aryan ideal. That included the handicapped, the homosexual and coloured communities, gypsies, Jehovah's Witnesses and those deemed to be 'asocial' – socialists, democrats and trade unionists.

'Guten Morgen young man,' Mathias greeted Jozef in Berlin university's dining hall. 'Do you mind, dear chap?'

Jozef did not have time to answer before Mathias seated himself and greedily began wolfing cereal and milk before looking forward to bacon and eggs. Mathias certainly ate well. Most students did at breakfast. First year undergraduates were left to fend for themselves at lunchtime, but were given breakfast and supper back at their halls to calm paranoid mothers' fears that they weren't feeding their sons or daughters properly.

Evening meals, invariably, were awful – cold, lumpy stews, poorly seasoned quickly killed appetites, except on Saturdays when 'snack suppers' were served of sausage and *salzkartoffeln*, which of course everyone devoured happily. Breakfasts, on the other hand, were spectacular. You could eat as much as you wanted. Crisp cereal; cold milk; hot porridge; and a feast of cooked luxuries – sausage, bacon, fried eggs and black pudding.

It certainly did not pay to sleep in – unless one could afford to eat out on an evening. Some could but not Jozef, who painstakingly eked out a shoestring weekly budget, enough to buy bread and cheese for lunch – and supper if needs be – and five pints of beer on a Friday night. He was usually sick after his fourth. No matter. The fact that he could afford a fifth kept him going through the week. Maybe this week he would manage it. Maybe you shouldn't try, Jozef imagined his mother warning him with half a smile back home.

Jozef had left his appetite back in Munich and had quickly lost weight in those first few days away, weight his slight but beautiful frame could ill afford to shed. His broad shoulders and slim stomach were beginning to look gaunt and turn in on themselves. Jozef was quite enjoying the emaciated look. He wrongly felt he had previously been carrying too much puppy fat.

'You never miss breakfast do you?' asked Mathias rhetorically from across the table the two of them uncomfortably shared.

The sun poured into the vast dining hall, abuzz with activity and spirits warmed by good food. A trickle of porridge slid distastefully from the right side of Mathias' mouth. He had not noticed and Jozef was not about to inform him.

'Are you a robot dear chap?'

Jozef was instantly offended. 'No,' he said simply, trying hard to remain polite.

The first year outcasts shuffled meekly by to take their usual table at the back of the dining hall. There was a pecking order even here and they instinctively knew their place at the bottom of it.

Jozef felt drawn to one of them – a girl with milk-bottomed glasses, which distorted her face unfavourably, but who was probably very pretty otherwise. Her skin, hidden by a conservative skirt and socks pulled up to her knees, was whiter than snow. She trailed behind the hardcore group of six outcasts, all boys, and it was clear she sensed she did not quite belong. But she did not know where else to go. It was early days, Jozef agreed in his head and then stopped himself from holding an imaginary conversation with her and refocused his attention to the plateful in front of him. He was ravenous.

CHAPTER ELEVEN

The Diederichs were having Karl and Jana Gottlieb, Sebastian's parents, over for dinner. It had been more than a year. The Gottliebs were unsure, but Catharina had suggested it and Jana did not have the heart to reject her proposal based on her female intuition. She could hear an SOS in the cracks of Catharina's voice. Jana knew Gerhard had the makings of a monster when drink took hold and was not about to abandon her acquaintance now. Karl had strongly advised that they make their excuses, even after Jana's initial acceptance, but Jana stayed true to their commitment. Gerhard hardly wanted the Gottliebs over either, but at least saw an opportunity to drink on such an occasion. His wife would not dare reproach him while they were entertaining.

The following morning Catharina was up early, tidying things away. Gerhard was still asleep. Last night had not been a success. Gerhard had been too drunk too early, but more than that – the whole evening had seemed wrong from the moment they had greeted the Gottliebs at the door. Their sons no longer lived in each other's pockets and without that bond tying the quartet together there was little will on either side to maintain good relations. What was the point, thought Gerhard through his stupor. Catharina had broken down while preparing dessert in the kitchen. Jana had followed and comforted her quietly. Catharina found the idea of homosexuality abhorrent, but in that delicate exchange she enjoyed more affection in Jana's kind caresses than in years of marriage.

'If you ever need me,' Jana said softly in her ear between gentle sobs. 'Just call round and we can talk, just talk.'

Catharina had nodded in reply while holding a dessert spoon and small pot of pouring cream, which caught one of her tears. 'I should throw this out,' Catharina said.

'Nonsense,' said Jana with a smile, which Catharina soon returned. 'Pouring cream. Nonsense.'

The two ladies served dessert back in the dining room together. Karl was relieved to see them. Gerhard had wanted to talk about the war again. Karl had had enough. It was time to look forward, he thought.

Life seemed hopeless for Catharina, who had started to accept that final fact. She had been happy once, but it had been so fleeting that she had not realised until the magic had disappeared like gold dust down a river. She looked back on that part of her life now like it belonged to a different person in a different time. She was an aging, dutiful wife. Her son had left home and so had laughter. If Catharina got through an evening without feeling like harming her husband it was something of a success. In her head, she was alone. Perversely, those were the kindest moments; the rest were simply to be endured.

Then, something happened.

The magic was back, unannounced like all those years before. She met someone and felt like she was fifteen again.

He worked at the butcher's on Georg-Elser-Platz and was younger than her but not too young. He was beautiful. He welcomed her from behind the counter, smiling disarmingly like only he could. It was not quite love at first sight, but something in her stirred and she loosened the collar of her scarf with lonely fingers.

'Guten Morgen Frau Diederich,' said Janus, who was Polish with elegant, dark hair swept over to one side.

'Guten Morgen,' said Catharina. There was no one else in the shop. It was only a few feet from the front door to a feast of meat separating Janus from her like a no man's land. He looked unreachable behind the counter with an apron smartly hugging his waist below a crisp T shirt.

'Herr Fleischer said to expect you,' said Janus. 'Two small pieces of steak, isn't it?'

'That's right,' said Catharina, who felt a happy flush of endorphins flooding her frame from below.

Catharina visited her butcher's twice a week, every week – once on Tuesdays to buy two pieces of steak for supper that evening and once on Thursdays to purchase two cheaper pork chops for the same purpose. It was part of Catharina's routine, part of her life and now it seemed that existence was being tossed up into the air to fall where it may. The uncertainty was unnerving but thrilling in the same breath. Years had built up, slowly depressing Catharina's heart like a skyscraper of tombs reaching impossibly high. Now, twice a week, every week, Janus was carefully lifting those dusty volumes away.

'Did you speak to anyone interesting today darling?' Gerhard said that evening over steak and potatoes and sad green beans, which Catharina had over boiled.

'No, not really,' she answered.

Catharina had forgotten what Janus looked like by the time she fell asleep that night, but her subconscious recalled him vividly in her dreams. She was walking slowly down country lanes. They were flanked by tall hedges which protected them from the glare of sunlight, which instead filtered through magically. She and Janus held hands, but Catharina was conscious the time they were spending together was painfully thin. The mood of her dream then darkened as quickly as the sky. Light muddied to dusk and Janus shrank by her side into a little boy while she looked away at the flickering sunset through the hedge.

'Jozef,' Catharina said when she woke.

CHAPTER TWELVE

It was Friday night in undergraduate halls and Jozef felt alive and ready to go out drinking in Berlin. He could hear records playing, friends laughing and sharing a beer or a bottle of wine – happiness. Jozef's own good mood was still tempered by depression. He was lonely. He had no one to share his anticipation of life with and the strong emotional conflict within him was something he had not previously experienced.

It was the end of week five, halfway through the first university term. Jozef was still friendless. He had settled in relatively well, he felt. He had sunk his teeth into his course and he was on top of his work, which if truth be told bored him slightly. He wanted, no, he expected, to be taxed more in higher education. He had feared he would be overwhelmed intellectually, but instead it was the opposite. He craved something more. Maybe I will speak with Professor Zielinski, Jozef thought as he combed his hair that evening. He pulled on the little light above the mirror with a cheap click to get a clearer picture. The main light in the centre of his room only reached dimly into its corners. The sudden illumination highlighted how dusty his mirror had become and Jozef wiped it clean with his handkerchief. That was better.

It was 7.30pm. He was wearing his smartest casuals and a deep green tweed jacket his mother had bought him as a going away present. The gesture, saved until his parents had said goodbye and left him alone in Berlin, had triggered a tidal wave of emotion. It had flooded up his legs and then his torso before finally filling his head until he overflowed with sadness. Jozef had hopelessly tried to hold it back, like a tiny figure facing a tsunami. Catharina had been distraught. Gerhard too had wanted to cry and had not expected to feel such emotion, but refrained in the final seconds, instead helping his wife deal with her upset.

Jozef waved them off, with water trickling down his cheeks, invisible in the darkness, the first cracks in the dam. He had held his jacket up triumphantly to his mother, who had smiled and reassured her son that her boy would be alright in all this – this life at university.

Jozef now made a final check he had the rest of his weekly budget in his pocket, safely protected ahead of tonight's spree, and locked the door to his room behind him. He put the key in his left pocket, which slipped beneath a handkerchief he always carried, whether he had a head cold or not. It had become habit. His right pocket exclusively held his money and it hearteningly jangled in his sharp grey pants. He felt attractive and his face smiled.

Mathias' door, across the hallway, was wide open as usual. Mathias spied Jozef coming out while he drank wine and entertained guests of both sex, which irked Jozef, who thought in the scheme of things his share of first year friends had been stolen by Mathias, who had enough for two or even three undergraduates. Martyn, a rich foreign undergraduate who lived next door to Jozef, came out at the same time and in the same conscientious manner locked his door and put the key safely in his trouser pocket. Martyn had soft red hair and was in one of Jozef's seminars – European Power Politics 1871-1914. He smiled at Jozef, who returned the compliment but felt unsure still.

Jozef walked up the narrow corridor.

Martyn's head surged. He wanted to invite Jozef to join them drinking. He had thought about doing so for the last week, but he had not found the right opportunity. This was it, he thought. 'Jozef!' he cried.

Jozef seemed decent and he instinctively felt that they would get along. He was not like other undergraduates. He spoke less and yet it was always worth listening to what he said. He talked with intelligence and made his arguments accessible, rather than wrapping them in words Martyn did not fully understand. Martyn was drowning intellectually, like he had feared all summer. His plea now made Mathias look up from the cosy party being conducted in his room across the hallway.

Jozef continued striding through the double doors and away to the left. The sound had not carried.

Monday morning and Jozef sat, as usual, alone in lectures. He liked it that way. No distractions. It was the busiest of the four courses he was taking this year – The Fall and Rise of Inter-War Germany 1919-1933.

Seductive, yes, but it seemed patently clear the university would really rather stop when Adolf Hitler had become chancellor.

'Let's leave it there, shall we?' Jozef pictured university chiefs deciding behind discreet doors.

It was 9am and grey and chilly outside. Buses and trams could not operate safely without their headlights on. Jozef was sat in the university's main lecture hall. There was nowhere else on campus which could happily host the 100-plus undergraduates gathered. Jozef felt awake, fresh. The main lecture hall banked steeply up from below where professors took centre stage and preached from their pulpit. The worn wooden boards were too big and grand for less skilful lecturers, Jozef thought in the opening weeks of term. A small stand held lecturers' notes at eye-level and a modest lamp shone on them on days like today.

Jozef felt safe but still close enough to the speaker, not too removed. He was an undergraduate and starting to feel rather proud of the fact.

A young man yawned openly a few rows down from Jozef. He was quickly admonished by the irritated professor giving today's lecture. 'Do that again, without using a hand to cover your mouth young man, and you can go and yawn somewhere else,' barked the professor, who was perhaps in his 40s and wearing a grey, thick beard.

Jozef made a mental note – hold yawns in, which always made Jozef feel like he was trying not to regurgitate a small mammal, wriggling alive.

'Adolf Hitler was 24 in 1913,' began the professor. 'He lived in Munich, but he was Austrian by birth. He struggled to get by selling drawings of local landmarks to tourists. He was bitter he could not make a better living from being an artist. A flatmate at the time remarked that Hitler was angry then and would 'pour fury over everything'.'

Jozef was scribbling notes voraciously with his best fountain pen, which smudged a little while the ink was still fresh. Few undergraduates took notes quite so conscientiously and Jozef was beginning to realise as much, but no matter. Jozef preferred to have too much information and sift out less vital snippets when it came to writing his essays. The formula was labour intensive but working for him so far. His lowest mark had been 59 out of 100, a C+ in old money. The majority of his work had scored in the low 60s, a B-.

'In May 1919, immediately after the end of the Great War, Hitler was desperate to remain in the German army. He was devastated the war had been lost. A Captain Karl Mayr came across him at the time and remarked how Hitler was 'like a stray dog, looking for a master'. Mayr saw something in Hitler. He felt he could work in propaganda and sent him to university in Munich to take a short course in public speaking. Hitler was 30 and now began to articulate his views in public, initially to German soldiers, about the dangers of communism.'

Jozef looked up. His wrist was starting to ache from writing so intensively. He waggled it quickly to try and shake off the numbing paralysis and adjusted his jacket, which had slipped uncomfortably into a crumpled pile behind the small of his back. He suddenly spotted Mathias below sat smugly between two attractive girls, one blonde, one brunette. What was he doing here and so early? Mathias did not like early mornings and was reading German literature, not modern history.

Jozef noticed Mathias spent an uncomfortable amount of time around girls. It seemed obvious to Jozef that he was sweet on most of them and if not them, then their best friend. His motives always seemed selfish. Mathias and the two girls were giggling and did not appear overly interested in what was being said. Jozef's conscience could not help tutting.

The professor finished his glass of water.

'Hitler began speaking in beer halls in Munich in 1919 and soon got noticed. People were angry after the defeat in the war and wanted someone to blame. Here was someone telling them who – communists and Jews.'

The next day Jozef had a seminar with Professor Zielinski and six other undergraduates on his course. He had lectures every week, but seminars only once a fortnight. That equalled six timetabled hours a week. The rest of the day Jozef was left to manage himself, wading through long reading lists and tirelessly producing the not insubstantial essays his courses demanded each month. The fact that no one from the university policed the students to ensure they were diligently doing their work was the downfall of those who lacked discipline.

Jozef was blossoming. He relished the independence of managing his days and applying himself when he was most alert, first thing in the morning and through the early part of the afternoon. A lot of undergraduates ploughed on through the evenings, but Jozef could not work at night.

This morning Jozef was first to knock on Professor Zielinski's door.

'Guten Morgen Jozef,' the professor said.

'Guten Morgen,' answered Jozef, who liked Professor Zielinski.

He had a kind, round face and was of average height and weight, but that was where averageness stopped and charming idiosyncrasy took over. The professor was in his 50s, Jozef guessed. His curly mop of hair was coiled tightly and his smile was disarming with a hint of rebellion about it. Jozef enjoyed the combination. He was the first person he had come across who could hold a candle to Herr Slupski, his old German teacher in Munich.

'How are you today?' asked the professor, fiddling with a bow tie, which clashed with his tweed jacket. Scruffy brown shoes let the professor down a little, but clearly he did not care and confidence hid a hundred flaws, thought Jozef, who was struggling to master that mindset. At university confidence was king and the currency most undergraduates traded in.

Jozef looked about himself after settling into his seat. He enjoyed Professor Zielinski's cluttered office with whole book cases teetering up instead of walls. It felt lived in. Jozef was five minutes early, an eternity for some undergraduates who timed entrances to the second, not wishing to invite extra work upon themselves. Small talk was required to avoid the interval quickly becoming uncomfortable.

'How are you finding university Jozef?'

Jozef felt like being honest. 'Gut. Tough at first, being away from home, but gut. I'm happy I feel I'm in the swing of things now workwise. I was worried I wouldn't...' Jozef broke off, searching for the right words.

'Be intelligent enough?' suggested the professor.

'Be intelligent enough,' repeated Jozef smiling. He wasn't entirely sure they were the exact words he would have chosen, but the professor had chosen them and they were good enough all the same.

Jozef sat opposite Professor Zielinski in the circle of chairs prepared to, one, encourage debate, but, two, because physically there was little choice – unless the professor was going to tidy up properly. He shuddered at the thought, like someone had just walked across his grave. It was bitter outside but beautiful. The professor had pulled down a blind to block sunlight from a modest window looking out of his office. Another showed a clear, blue sky like the sea.

'I like to think that being conscious of one's own shortcomings is in itself a higher form of intelligence,' noted the professor.

Jozef nodded gently in agreement. 'I'd never thought of it like that,' he said.

'How are you finding the work?' probed the professor, sipping his coffee. Tiny wisps of smoke weaved up out of his mug.

'Work's okay. I have to be honest, I thought it might be tougher. I feel I want more; I want to know more,' said Jozef.

'What about?' asked the professor, puzzled.

'About Adolf Hitler, about National Socialism and about what they did in the death camps,' said Jozef suddenly.

'The death camps you say,' said the professor, raising an eyebrow. 'How do you know they even existed?'

'I suppose I don't – but I'd like to,' said Jozef.

A fellow undergraduate then bundled through the door, gasping for breath and hurriedly unwrapping a scarf from around her neck. 'Sorry I'm late professor,' she said.

'No problem. Myself and young Jozef here were just enjoying a meeting of minds.'

Jozef was flattered but didn't grasp the professor's full meaning. The girl was jealous and frowned before burying her hands into one of a clutch of bags and producing a pen and worn notebook.

'Shall we begin?' said the professor.

CHAPTER THIRTEEN

'Guten Morgen Frau Diederich,' said Janus from behind the counter.

There was another customer ahead of her peeking at the meat but failing to make a decision. Catharina found herself silently riling at the woman, who was wearing a scarf which cloaked her irritating head, ducking and fussing about. Her own anger surprised Catharina. She could not help wanting Janus all to herself. Janus seemed to mirror the sentiment, smiling when he caught her eye and half rolling his in jest at the other woman's indecision.

Catharina tried desperately to not let the woman spoil her mood, which had been brilliant upon first entering the shop. She had been excited. She wanted to be buoyant for her, however brief, exchange with him – but the woman continued to dally between decisions. Catharina would have gladly handed her over to the Gestapo had the war still been on. She certainly looked like she might have 'Jewish tendencies'.

'Will the ham keep?' asked the lady.

'Of course it will,' Janus replied.

Catharina was forced to hover awkwardly behind.

'And the sausages?'

'The sausages will keep as well.'

Finally. The lady scuttled out of the shop tucking the meat carefully in her bag, which she seemed almost to crouch over as an added layer of protection.

Catharina breathed a sigh of relief and returned her focus to Janus and she held his look. She had not studied his face closely before. She had been too embarrassed to do so. Now she did, Janus seemed more comfortable in the intimacy of the moment, more confident of his looks.

'Alone at last,' Catharina joked.

Janus laughed and Catharina was thrilled. She couldn't recall the last time she had made someone happy.

She fantasised about Janus in bed before falling asleep that night. She imagined what he might do to her and what she might do to him, exploring soft, nude skin. It only felt more thrilling knowing that her husband lay right next to her and had no idea what was racing through her head. Catharina's mind was running away from her. All too brief dalliances in the butcher's, potentially in front of other people, people Catharina was acquainted with, were not enough anymore, nowhere near. She pictured how she might take her relationship with Janus further. She was becoming quietly convinced Janus felt the same way. The smiles were returned too quickly from across the counter in the shop, too warmly, for her not to be right.

This was a second chance in love. Catharina had to try and take it. The alternative filled her only with emptiness; the alternative was growing old with Gerhard, who she could never forgive. Catharina considered waiting for Janus to leave work one day and approaching him when she knew he would be free of other people. She thought about inviting him out while buying meat one day, although that was both dangerous – the shop owner, who Gerhard knew, could quite easily hear – and terrifying. Catharina would not be able to live with herself if she faltered and fluffed her lines. Her entire happiness was on the line.

She thought about secretly passing Janus a note along with her money. This idea was terrifying too, but also the most appealing. She could articulate exactly what she wanted and how she wanted to say it. Janus would get the message. The answer was then up to him. Catharina's conscience at least would be safely beyond reproach if it was a crushing no.

The next evening, she sat at her bedroom cabinet holding a pen over an empty sheet of possibilities. The mahogany cabinet was grand, rather too grand, for the modest surroundings it found itself in in their bedroom. Still, Catharina was fond of it. Gerhard had bought it for her when times were better. She cast her gaze down wistfully for a moment. Catharina's loneliness lay around her bare feet like petals. She was 17 again and writing a love letter. She could not quite believe her boldness.

. . .

Dear Janus,

Forgive me. Please meet me for a drink on Thursday evening, 8pm, at Rudolf's on Cathedral Street. Catharina Diederich

She tried to be as brief as possible. She wanted to fold what she had written into a tiny parcel that could easily be passed to Janus when she paid her bill. She had considered writing 'Janus, I think I am falling in love with you' but thought this message might intrigue him more. Catharina carefully put down her pen and faintly fragranced the paper with perfume. This was not a time to hold back. She would deliver it tomorrow and then have until next Thursday to discover Janus' true intentions. The excitement of a potential meeting would carry her through she was sure.

She began folding the piece of paper, first in half and then into quarters and finally in half again. There. She glanced up at the mirror curving around the top of the bedroom cabinet and caught her own eyes, like she was trying to scare herself. She looked so serious. She immediately smiled self-deprecatingly. For once that night, she went to bed after her husband. Catharina had had to go downstairs and spotlessly tidy the kitchen before finally starting to come down emotionally. Gerhard knew it was unusual. He felt her frame shift beside him and stirred back to consciousness.

'Everything okay, darling?' he slurred.

'Everything is fine. Go back to sleep, sweetheart,' she said, kissing the back of his head.

She felt proud of herself if the truth be told. She felt in charge of her life again. It was 1959 after all. Why couldn't a woman ask a man out?

CHAPTER FOURTEEN

Mathias' father scurried through a claustrophobic corridor to answer the telephone. It was late. He sensed with some portent who it could be. Michael. He picked up the red telephone thick with dust and diligently began wiping it down as he brought it up to his ear. Mathias' father was a career citizen. He had blown with the storm which had raged across mainland Europe throughout the 1930s and 1940s – unpredictable and frightening. You never quite knew if the gale was set in for the night or whether it was about to suddenly blow itself out.

Mathias' father had been a rare ally in the Catholic Church for the Nazis during their twelve years in power. He had been jealous of the Jews and their success and had been perfectly happy for his young family to join the far right.

'Guten Abend,' he said into the now clean red telephone.

'Heinrich, it's Michael.'

'Hello Michael,' said Mathias' father brightly despite the late hour and deep fatigue flagging his mood. 'How are you this evening?'

'I'm fine. I'm going to have to lean on you some more, old friend. You do understand?'

'Of course, of course,' repeated Mathias' father.

'I need Mathias to take a closer interest in Jozef at university. Certain forces would like to know more about his time away from home, you understand.'

'Yes, yes, of course, Michael.'

He put the telephone down and immediately rang his son. Mathias was not happy to be hauled out of bed by the doorman at this hour.

The following morning, Jozef had a lecture in the main theatre. The sky was grey and ominous, but, because of its blanket, the bite had been softened in the January air. Jozef was walking down the hill into the heart of the campus with a large flock of undergraduates busy jostling and jockeying for position. The effort of crawling out of bed early, for them at least, would have been wasted if they arrived late. Some had slices of toast in hungry mouths. Others clasped large volumes and files close to their chest. Jozef carried a cheap, brown briefcase. It was hardly dashing but it served its purpose and Jozef was growing to rather like it. He felt almost statesmanlike. Suddenly, a strong arm reached around his shoulder.

'Guten Morgen, old friend,' said Mathias popping up sharply on Jozef's flank.

'Guten Morgen, Mathias,' Jozef said, struggling to free himself of his unwanted friend's grip.

'I didn't think you had anything first thing?'

'I don't,' said Mathias. 'I'm coming with you to history. You don't mind, old man?' It was like they were long lost pals.

'No,' lied Jozef, who certainly did. Jozef felt lonely on Friday nights when he didn't have anyone to share a beer with but not on Monday mornings when he had lectures. Then he treasured the solitude. Jozef had quietly determined to never become one of those undergraduates who required a crop of friends permanently surrounding them at class, smoking cigarettes in-between lectures and making university life look effortless. If Jozef, finally wriggling free of Mathias' grip, made it look hard and lonely, he thought, it was because it was hard and lonely, at least for him.

'Guten Morgen,' announced a professor walking onto the stage and into the pulpit below.

'Do you always sit this close in lectures?' whispered Mathias.

'Yes, I like to sit this close.'

'Today we are going to talk about Adolf Hitler,' began the professor. 'And the rise in his popularity through the 1920s until he became chancellor in 1933. Intellectuals have assumed that Hitler was a hugely charismatic man, who seduced the German people and who was always bound to lead. The Nazis and the Second World War come 1939 were inevitable. There was nothing we, the people, could do against that great force. I would argue otherwise.'

Jozef liked that the professor was not afraid to swim against the tide.

'Jesus, Jozef, do you always make this many notes?' complained Mathias, who Jozef had briefly but happily forgotten was there.

'Yes, I always take this many notes,' said Jozef pointedly.

Mathias got the hint. 'Okay, okay,' he said and Jozef felt better for defending his stance for once.

Mathias was beginning to regret coming and scanned the theatre for eligible young women. There were too many to count.

Jozef then noticed the unfashionable girl from his halls sat on her own beneath him.

'This is testimony from someone at the time. They said, "Hitler uttered what was in the consciousness of everyone present". He uttered what was in the consciousness of everyone present,' the professor repeated.

'I would argue Hitler did not spellbind people before and after he became chancellor in 1933. He simply told them what they wanted to hear. Times were tough in Germany in the 1920s, but people were not ashamed or guilty like they feel now following a Second World War. People were angry after the Great War and needed someone to blame – Jews.'

Jozef's right wrist started to ache dully from writing so furiously. Today, whenever he came up for air in moments like this, he immediately recalled Mathias' uncomfortable presence to his left.

Mathias then broke wind suddenly. 'Sorry,' he said smiling.

Jozef couldn't help smirking also. It was the first time Mathias had amused him.

'After Hitler's call for a national revolution in Munich in 1923 he spent some time in prison where he wrote *Mein Kampf*,' continued the professor, assuming a static position at the centre of the stage. 'In it he wrote, "We have broken the laws of natural selection. We have supported unworthy life forms and we have allowed them to breed".'

It was Friday night and Jozef was looking forward to a drink. He had grown used to not having company on Friday evenings and he had come to enjoy them more, despite the pangs of loneliness which pulled at the corners of his mood.

A knock at the door. Mathias.

'Hello,' said Jozef, more comfortable around the undergraduate who lived opposite him now.

'All dressed up I see, but where are you going?' asked Mathias, mildly drunk.

'Just out.'

'Just out. You're a mysterious one, aren't you?'

Mathias was backed by Martyn, the Danish undergraduate from next door, who smiled at Jozef, and also by Pierre, who was already too intoxicated to do anything but sway unsteadily on his feet in time with his long hair. Pierre was from Elsaß-Lothringen, the west quarter of Germany which had briefly belonged to France in the 1920s and 1930s following Germany's defeat in the Great War.

'Would you like to come out with us?' Martyn asked politely.

Jozef felt a surge of excitement jolt through his veins. Week six and finally – finally – he was going out with people he had met at university. 'One minute!' he exclaimed.

Mathias was satisfied. He knew his father would be pleased and he would now get to know the real Jozef Diederich, he thought. He would at the very least be able to report back with some authority.

Martyn and Pierre too were pleased. They had become rather tired of Mathias dominating their trio on evenings out.

Jozef's mind was a happy whirlwind, chaotic but blissful. He slapped the outside of his left trouser pocket and felt a handkerchief and his room key, and in his right trouser pocket he felt Deutsche Marks. Everything he needed. He whirled back around to face Mathias, Martyn and Pierre, who was starting to come round a little.

'Right, I'm ready.'

'Let's go then,' answered Mathias with a smile.

'Where are we going?' asked Jozef as the four undergraduates strode out of their halls on a mission to drink and find fun.

'We're going over to the other side,' said Mathias cryptically. 'East Berlin.'

'East Berlin!' said Jozef startled. 'We're not really going there, are we?'

'We're really going there, old man,' repeated Mathias, calmly lighting his first cigarette of the evening before handing one to Pierre, who would smoke like a chimney if only he could afford to. Instead, he cadged smokes whenever he could, Jozef noticed. Mathias smoked more for the look. Pierre hungrily inhaled big drags on his cigarettes, before grinding out the stubs on the concrete with the soul of his black boot, which fitted incongruously with his softer temper.

'Relax,' said Mathias. 'We simply get the tube to the east. I'm fully aware it's illegal but the police don't care. Everyone does it. Thousands flock to the west through Berlin. It's the last loophole between the sectors. My father says they'll try and close the border here one day.'

Jozef took his ally's advice and tried to relax. He began talking to Martyn and happily soon realised that they shared a love for football and the cinema. They supported FC Bayern Munich and had both played

60

football in their youth, although it seemed clear Jozef had been a much better player. Mathias, although you wouldn't have guessed from his decadent habits and obsession with women, too was a huge football fan but liked less fashionable teams and lectured tiringly about the arrogance of the big, powerful clubs. Pierre could usually see both sides of an argument and smiled at Jozef. The pair of them had shared a connection since the look they had exchanged that first evening when Jozef, spinning with homesickness, had rejected their invitation to go drinking. Jozef finally felt vindicated in that decision and began to feel rather proud of himself that patience had brought its reward.

They paused for a beer in one of the busiest pubs in Berlin before turning off the hectic strip and into the darker backstreets. The roars of the main public houses in town grew quieter as they walked down the hill to the subway to the east and the Soviet sector. The first glass of alcohol of the evening had gone straight to Jozef's and Martyn's heads. Neither of them were seasoned socialites like Mathias and Pierre.

Jozef still felt uneasy about what he was about to do. What would his parents say? Munich and the safe life he had led for 18 years suddenly seemed a world away. Berlin was buzzing and the night beckoned intoxicatingly before them. Jozef was comforted by Martyn's and Pierre's presence. If they were going it must be okay, he thought. Mathias still irritated Jozef, but, it was true, the four of them formed a happy crowd. The chemistry was right. Nobody dominated. Everyone felt comfortable in the larger context.

'What's in the east?' said Jozef to Martyn, who he was sticking to like glue.

Mathias, five yards ahead with Pierre and his cigarettes for company, turned around. 'Jazz, old boy. Bebop to be precise.'

Jozef's musical tastes were conservative at best. He had never heard of it. 'Beeebop,' he said slowly, trying to wrap his mind around it.

The group reached the subway station and bought tickets for East Berlin. Jozef felt hugely conspicuous buying his and was the last of them to do so. His anxious face flushed hot despite the chill. All he could think about while the guard took his money was that he must know what he was up to. He must know.

Of course the guard did. The four boys – because they were still just boys – stood out at this time on a Friday night smelling of liquor, but the guard didn't care. He wasn't paid enough to. He dismissively gave Jozef his ticket and looked immediately to his right.

Jozef still dare not move, waiting to be dismissed almost like he was back at school.

Mathias walked up to the shabby counter and put his arm around his companion. 'Come on, Jozef,' he said. 'We can go now.'

Jozef smiled back at Mathias. It was the first time the two of them had really shared a moment. It may have been partly fuelled by alcohol and illicit thrill, but it was true all the same.

Jozef broke free from Mathias and ran forward to Martyn and embraced him excitedly. The four of them were on their way. Jozef's first real adventure at university was finally beginning.

CHAPTER FIFTEEN

Catharina looked at herself in the mirror. It was a grey, anonymous morning, but that didn't alter the fact that this was more than just another day. She was about to try to commit adultery. Even though she felt the moral high ground in her marriage was hers, a court of law, she was sure, would not quite view it that way. Gerhard would get everything and even, perhaps, Jozef. But Jozef was gone now. She wasn't sure he was ever coming back.

Rain started falling, tapping increasingly quickly on the window outside. She grimaced, annoyed. She would have to wear a headscarf. Catharina would have really rather not – her hair looked attractive today and for that she was thankful – but rain would transform her into a drowned cat. The lesser of two choices was always obvious to her. She shared that trait with Jozef, while Gerhard could never see the world so clearly. Choices seemed hard for him. Catharina tried to wonder what that must be like, to not know your own mind, but she couldn't make the empathetic leap in her head.

Catharina looked down at her hand and in its palm she cradled her letter, tightly swaddled like a baby. She had put so much heart into it. Despite last-minute nerves unsettling her motivation, she had to go through with her plan of action now. She closed the front door behind her and looked up at the sky overhead. The rain had sounded worse inside. It was only a heavy drizzle once out in it. Still, the headscarf, her favourite flowery one, had to stay on. She walked quickly down the short path leading to her front gate with her shopping bag tucked tightly under her arm. She was going to the butcher's first, even though normally she would visit there last. She couldn't function if she didn't get this letter out of her possession. It was too explosive to sit there loaded for long.

She approached the butcher's and quickly tidied herself, running her hands down her skirt and loosening her headscarf. The sun was beginning to peak out. The shop was packed when she arrived. Catharina quickly spied Janus' handsome face behind an army of wives all clamouring to be served the best meat in the store.

Janus spotted Catharina in between serving and returned her look of comic distress at the chaos separating them. Janus rolled glinting eyes, which immediately returned her mood to last night's thrilling heights.

She was sure she was doing the right thing and that she was not misreading the signals they had been sending each other. Catharina steadied her emotions as best she could. She was so excited she did not mind waiting today. She was happy to bide her time and mentally prepare before handing over her note. She had deliberately worn thin layers because she knew she was liable to perspire under pressure. Her temperature began to rise the closer her moment to being served came.

'Hello Frau Diederich. How are you today?'

'Catharina, please,' she said. 'I think I should be asking how you are after dealing with all that.'

'Ha!' Janus exclaimed, laughing. 'I am fine. I am used to them. They are no problem,' he said in broken German.

Catharina loved it when his Polish roots flavoured his accent. 'Rather you than me,' Catharina said, laughing nervously and suddenly hating herself for doing so.

'The usual, Frau Diederich? Two smaller pieces of fillet steak?'

'Janus,' Catharina gently reprimanded.

'The usual, Catharina?' Janus tried again, soothing her nerves like the butterfly kisses she had dreamt him giving her.

'The usual, Janus,' she said.

This was it. She peered down into her palm and carefully placed the tightly folded piece of paper behind her money and handed the precious pile to Janus. She was doing it, she exclaimed in her head, without quite believing it. It felt like an out of body experience.

'Keep the change,' she said quickly before grabbing the meat from Janus and racing out of the shop.

'Frau Diederich!' he called after her, reverting back to formality now the pair of them had broken the intimacy of eye contact.

Catharina's heart was thumping so heavily in her chest she might have missed an atomic bomb crushing central Munich.

'You have given me too much,' said Janus, his voice trailing off.

He could see Catharina had been going somewhere in a hurry. Then he noticed she hadn't made a mistake.

Catharina could not eat that evening.

'Are you okay, darling?' asked Gerhard, sat across from her. 'You've hardly touched your food.'

'I'm fine, sweetheart,' replied Catharina. 'I was just thinking about Jozef and how he's settling in Berlin. That's all.'

'I'm sure he's fine, darling, absolutely fine. We've talked about this. We have to let Jozef be himself now. That's why we decided to tell him he's adopted, to give him time to think and let him return to us naturally.'

The truth was they had not decided that the eve of Jozef's departure for Berlin was the right time to reveal he was adopted. Gerhard had decided and there was nothing Catharina could have said to dissuade him.

'What if he never comes back to us?' said Catharina, suddenly tearful and angry at the thought.

Gerhard said nothing, irate at the interruption.

'Sorry, sweetheart. You're right,' she added. A second lie. Catharina had not been thinking about Jozef at all while she had initially played with her steak. She had been thinking of Janus and trying to fathom just what he might be considering eating his dinner this evening. He had her note! Catharina still could not quite believe it. She was so excited she did not feel she would eat at all until next Thursday when she would finally learn his answer. Catharina would have to go to the cafe and sit there and wait. It would be horrendous and heart-stopping in the same impossible breath.

CHAPTER SIXTEEN

The train into East Berlin was quiet. It felt like a one-way passage to the end of the Earth. No one seemed keen to arrive there. The train jerked clumsily to a halt and the four of them climbed off.

Jozef was keen to drink another beer. He was sobering up and he wanted another hit of alcohol.

Everything seemed grey in East Berlin.

Jozef wondered if before his death Stalin had banned colour. Everyone's coats were a drab brown or washed-out blue. People seemed miserable. There were no smiles, no laughter, only tension and a tangible police presence everywhere – the Stasi, which quickly made Jozef anxious again.

A Stasi officer caught his eye.

Paranoid, Jozef looked quickly at his shoes to avoid the glare.

Martyn was not overly confident either. Mathias was fine and lit another cigarette, while Pierre was too drunk to either notice or care and stuck close to Mathias, half bouncing off him if his balance gave way. He occasionally wiped the hair out of his face and tried to gather himself, but it was a poor impression of trying to appear sober. It seemed obvious to Jozef he was quite drunk. Still, Jozef found Pierre intriguing, charming even.

'We made it,' said Mathias, looking back over his shoulder.

Jozef half nodded and smiled, looking about himself and trying to take it all in. He remained convinced the four of them stuck out badly, but no one else seemed to mind, so why should he? he thought.

They bustled into a busy bar. The tight door jammed open into a bawdy crowd of people cloaked in smoke. The bar itself was down a narrow corridor flanked by dingy booths, which each squeezed in six patrons. A group of men and women were leaving and Pierre and Martyn quickly grabbed their booth.

Jozef followed Mathias to get served.

It was two-deep at the bar, but his companion knew how to discreetly jump the queue, sneaking in at one end.

'Four pints of beer, please,' Mathias shouted to the barwoman through the din. 'Here you go,' he continued, handing Jozef two tall glasses overflowing with strong beer.

'Thank you,' said Jozef.

He was looking forward to this. He fought the short way back to the booth and sat alongside Pierre, who was nearest the wall, while Mathias sat opposite Jozef next to Martyn.

'Cheers,' said Pierre raising his glass – but only after taking a large swig first – and the four friends merrily clinked their pints together in the centre of the table, spilling a little beer here and there.

A sexy brunette walked up to the bar and caught Jozef's eye. She smiled at him. He blushed. He felt like a child in this strange quarter of the city and way out of the woman's league.

Mathias noticed the silent exchange and made eyes at Jozef. He was happy but rather jealous and still could not work Jozef out. Was there more to him that he did not yet know?

'I have to go somewhere,' Mathias said.

'What? Where are you going?' said Jozef, anxious to keep the group together on his first foray into Berlin's Soviet sector.

'Don't worry,' said Mathias, draining the dregs of his beer and rising and wrapping his jacket around his shoulders. 'We'll meet you back here in an hour. Have a drink, relax.'

'Do you want another pint, Pierre?' Jozef asked.

Pierre nodded, squinting through cigarette smoke floating up from a final fag cadged from Mathias before he left.

Jozef took the hint. It was clear he was buying; it was becoming clear you were always buying with Pierre.

'Are you okay?' Jozef said to his new friend when he sat down with the two beers which had taken forever to buy. Jozef had finally paid the price for sticking out. West Berliners got served last in the Soviet sector.

'I'm fine Jozef,' Pierre said, more sober now and with perhaps his heaviest drinking behind him this evening.

'Where did Mathias go?' said Jozef.

'He went to see a girl. I can't remember her name,' said Pierre.

'Ah,' said Jozef. 'A girl.'

Pierre nodded again, glugging his way through the first half of his pint at an alarming speed. Jozef had only had two sips of his. Perhaps Pierre's heaviest drinking was not behind him this evening after all.

'Why did Martyn go?'

'I think he introduced the two of them through a girl he knows at university,' said Pierre.

Jozef nodded. 'It's nice to sit down and finally chat,' he said, trying to dilute any remaining discomfort between them.

'Yes, it's nice to finally sit down and chat with you too.'

The pair of them had common ground – not only from shared interests, but from a broader outlook on life. Pierre and Jozef had an understanding.

'It's been nearly an hour,' said Jozef. 'Shall we get another drink in?'

'Yes, same again, please.'

Jozef smiled. Pierre must be skint, he thought. It was hardly his fault – Jozef liked him – but if it had been Mathias claiming poverty, it might have been a different story, Jozef thought wryly.

An hour became an hour and a half and Jozef became concerned. He felt time sliding away dangerously, like the route back to the west might close on them forever.

'Is he always this late?'

'He can be – when a girl's involved. He'll know what time it is. Let's go.'

'Where?' asked Jozef. He didn't know anywhere else – only this place and the subway station home.

'Let's walk down the street and see what we can find,' said Pierre, like it was the most mundane thing in the world.

Jozef didn't want to wander anywhere. He wanted clear structure to this evening.

'Don't worry,' Pierre said. 'We can always walk home to the western sector. There are no barriers stopping us.'

He wrapped his arm fondly around Jozef, who was 6ft and taller than Pierre. It was an effort for him, which made him reach more heartily. It felt nice, thought Jozef, who was lovely and warm and drunk he realised, now out in the night air. His head swam happily.

'Is that the jazz club?' Jozef said, spying a dark doorway and two men standing guard outside.

They stood at a badly lit crossroads. The road swept round to their right and back up to the safety of the subway station and the west. To their left lay a smaller back road, leading nowhere at first glance. Immediately on their left, tucked around the bottom of the hill and away from prying eyes, was *Rolf's*, according to the pink neon letters glowing garishly above the door. The cheap sign had nothing in common with the burly pair of bouncers guarding the entrance beneath it.

'No, that's not the place,' said Pierre.

'Shall we try it?' said Jozef, trying to relax.

'Okay,' said Pierre, shrugging casually.

They each had to pay to enter the club. A squat man wearing a thick beard took their money. He was squeezed into a small cubicle which greeted revellers upon arrival, halfway down a flight of stairs. It sounded like an unbridled riot was taking place below. Hectic music, laughter, cheering and loud chatter. Two women wearing men's tuxedos bounced up the stairs past Jozef and Pierre.

At the bottom of the stairs was a long bar and a dance floor, crowded happily with couples and friends. One half of the room had seats and tables, but they were largely empty. Most people were dancing and having a fantastic time. There were men and women and groups of friends but no one like Jozef or Pierre on first impression.

Jozef felt uncomfortable.

Pierre lit a cigarette and started making his way over to the bar. 'What do you want to drink?' he asked. 'Beer?'

'Yes, beer,' yelled Jozef.

They passed two men melting their bodies together and French kissing deeply.

Jozef had never seen two men kissing before. Then he remembered the women on the stairs and looked again at the people dancing. He noticed nearly all of the couples were of the same sex.

'Pierre, Pierre!'

Pierre, with the cigarette in his mouth preventing him from speaking, motioned he was in the middle of getting served.

'There you go, handsome,' said the barman to Pierre, presenting him with two large glasses of beer.

'Thanks,' said Pierre routinely, ignoring the compliment.

He handed Jozef one of the beers and both of them drained a good third of their glasses with their first swig. Jozef was gasping slightly when he came up for air. He wanted the alcohol to make his mind swirl again – and quickly.

'Pierre!' Jozef said again like he was passing on state secrets. 'We're in a club for fairies.'

'I know,' said Pierre smiling.

'Did you know this was a club for fairies?'

'No, I didn't,' Pierre said, still amused.

'What are we going to do? I think we have to leave – but together. We can pretend we're a couple.'

'Relax. We've only just got here. Let's take a seat.'

Jozef quickly finished his drink and went back to the bar and bought two more beers. It was not like him to drink so quickly. He was beginning to lose track of how many he had had tonight. He was glad to return to the sanctuary of their table and his companion, who was smoking again.

'I didn't think you had any cigarettes?' said Jozef, surprised and enjoying his pint more slowly this time. He was starting to feel good again.

'I do,' Pierre shrugged, wiping away hair from his face, a common mannerism for him. 'I'm happy to cadge as many as I can from Mathias though. Don't tell him.'

Jozef felt flattered to receive the confession, however small. The people dancing were from another planet, he then thought – but he found himself growing to like them. They were not aggressive or spoiling for trouble, Jozef's big bugbear when he was out drinking in pubs and bars. He wished he was a closet lunatic when strange men caught his eye and tacitly challenged him on a night out. Leave me alone, his head screamed in those feverish moments. Here, there were no such unspoken challenges, although Jozef had noticed four men perched at the bar, quite apart from everyone else.

The strange men were haggard and immovable, like they lived on their bar stools. Their faces sank into themselves. Alcohol and nicotine abuse had drawn deep lines on their features, now struggling to prop up sagging flesh and there was a warm, pungent smell clouding them like fog, although they were only smoking cigarettes from what Jozef could tell.

'It's marijuana,' said Pierre. 'It's pretty common in jazz clubs in Berlin.'

'How do you know all this?'

'I just know,' said Pierre, shrugging again.

Jozef and Pierre were drunk in the jazz club that night. They got on famously like old friends and talked about football, movies, girls and each other. Pierre's parents were both big drinkers. At least Gerhard was a quiet one, Jozef thought to himself with some relief while he listened to his new friend open up.

After an intimidating start, Jozef loved *Rolf's*. He realised he liked homosexuals. They were fun; they didn't seem to care what anyone else thought or did. They were happy to live and let live. Cool, thought Jozef, who felt liberated watching them dance without inhibition to the frantic in-house jazz band. Jozef and Pierre joined them before the evening was out and the club closed at 3am. Jozef danced more than Pierre – he enjoyed more natural rhythm – and attracted the attention of others, mainly for his smooth motion but also for his kind face and good looks. Jozef was happy. He was at home. It was a small revelation to him.

The pair of them walked home. Jozef was glad to get back to the West and out of the Soviet sector. Others from *Rolf's* would have come too, but they had lives to lead – families, jobs, houses. The state keenly repressed the emergence of the homosexual community in post-war East Germany. But they did not mind. At least in East Germany homosexuality laws were not rigidly enforced – unlike the West, where the church was more influential. From 1957 in East Germany, homosexuality was quietly tolerated, just not openly encouraged. That was enough for the people who visited *Rolf's* every Friday. They had a few hours to be different, a few hours to be themselves.

Jozef was beginning to understand.

CHAPTER SEVENTEEN

'You look nice,' said Gerhard from behind his newspaper after supper. He was happy. He knew he was going to enjoy a drink tonight.

'Thank you, sweetheart,' said Catharina nervously. She felt uncomfortable dressed so well around her husband in the blandness of their home. She wanted to dive out into the night where her elegance might be more fitting and in keeping with others.

Her head was a whirlwind. She needed a drink. 'Would you mind if I had a glass of whisky?' she asked, hoping and praying she would not elicit intrigue.

She felt it was the most obvious thing in the world that she was bidding to embark upon an affair right under her husband's nose.

'Let's both have one,' agreed Gerhard gladly, rising from his seat and reaching inside their dining room cabinet to find a bottle of his best stuff. He grabbed two glasses from a cupboard and began pouring. Catharina got a small nip; Gerhard got a generous double. He could not help his selfishness when alcohol was involved. 'Prost,' said Gerhard, raising his glass after retaking his seat opposite his wife.

'Prost,' said Catharina, calming a little after her first sip, which made her throat burn but her hand steady.

'Is something special happening tonight at choir practice?' Gerhard asked, alluding to his wife's appearance.

'Yes. We're having group photos taken for publicity shots for shows coming up over the summer.'

Gerhard nodded and looked down again at his newspaper.

Catharina studied him intensely. She was looking for any hint of disbelief in his body language, but she could not find any and she started to relax more deeply. She checked the clock hanging high on the wall. 7pm. Half an hour before she was due to meet Janus – if he showed. Catharina had increasingly begun to think he would not. What a fool she had been, she thought. But she had to go now.

'Okay, darling,' said Catharina, looking at herself one last time in the mirror in their hallway. She needn't have. She had looked perfect on the previous three occasions she had checked herself in the last hour. 'I'll see you later.'

'Bye, darling,' said Gerhard, looking forward to her exit himself so he could begin drinking seriously, rather than politely sip his whisky.

Catharina enjoyed the first wave of cool evening air enveloping her after she closed the front door. It took the warm sting out of the panic she had experienced in the last few hours. She took a deep breath and ran both her hands down her dress. She checked her bag briefly to see that some money lay within it. It was a ten-minute walk to the café she had proposed for their rendezvous. She would be early for 7.30pm, but no matter. She preferred it that way. It gave her time to gather herself.

En route to the café, Catharina's senses were acutely aware of everything. The general chatter floating out from pubs as she paced by; the little giggles and whispers shared by lovers out strolling across the street; and the sound of night buses rushing up behind her or slowly approaching from ahead. Catharina heard it all like she had not heard it in years.

When she saw Janus was already seated in the café on the corner of the street, her heart did not simply skip a beat, it somersaulted in her pounding chest. She kept walking, desperately trying to ensure she was not seen. She had to. She had to compose herself from all this – breathlessness.

She flew past the café, which had fronts on both streets it cornered and, out of sight of its clientele, she picked up her feet and danced for half a moment. Catharina had not danced for a lifetime. Calm yourself, she reprimanded herself playfully. But she couldn't. She could hardly believe she was about to walk into a café and court another man. Another man. She was married. She didn't do this. She had never done this. It felt like the engagement she was about to experience would be savoured by another woman entirely – a confident, attractive, middle-aged woman perfectly happy to throw caution to life's wind before it rolled relentlessly by. She gathered herself. The café glowed romantically inside, lit magically by pockets of candlelight at each table. She opened the door and entered another world.

'Guten Abend. Are you alone this evening?' asked a waitress.

'No, I'm meeting someone, the gentleman sat over there,' said Catharina discreetly, motioning to Janus, who was seated alone and quite apart from other customers.

She carefully weaved her way through the maze of tables to him. 'Hello Janus.'

Catharina struggled to stop her heart from beating outside her thumping chest.

'Guten Abend, Frau Diederich,' said Janus stiffly to Catharina's disappointment.

'Janus, two things,' said Catharina with uncharacteristic boldness. 'First, let me order you another glass of wine – red? Second, you have to start calling me Catharina or we'll think we're still in the butcher's.'

'Catharina,' Janus nodded, acknowledging her self-deprecating request.

Catharina smiled. She climbed out of her raincoat and hung it on the back of her chair before sitting down. She ordered two glasses of red wine and composed herself, running her hands down her skirt – her favourite – to smooth out creases, which had the same effect upon her emotionally. 'This is lovely,' she said, looking around.

She was grateful for the dusky light. It hid the fact that she must be Janus' senior by ten years, give or take, but she didn't feel it tonight. She felt she had stopped living for entire chunks of the last decade.

'You look beautiful,' said Janus.

He was wearing a simple shirt, trousers and shoes. He was clearly not a rich man – but she did not care. Tonight, his kind eyes and soft manners were hers exclusively.

'Thank you,' she said, breaking eye contact and looking at her new shoes awkwardly. She was not used to praise, especially from someone she was so attracted to.

Janus was a hairy man and already his morning shave was overtaken by stubble. He kept his dark hair neat and tidy, and had a deep tan in contrast to Catharina's pale skin, which she was careful to protect from sunlight for fear of getting burnt.

The waitress carried over two glasses of blood red wine, balanced expertly on a tray. Catharina drank some of hers quickly.

'I received your letter, thank you,' said Janus, which unseated Catharina, who did not care to mention it.

'Oh,' said Catharina uncomfortably. 'I hope you didn't mind. I was trying to be discreet.'

'You were perfectly discreet.'

Catharina felt unnerved looking Janus directly in the eye.

He, conversely, appeared comfortable holding her gaze. He looked and smelt different free from the formality and everyday business of the butcher's. There, they had good reason to talk. Now, they had very different reasons.

She was glad and felt more attracted to him than ever. There was magic in the air across their table in the café that night. Every time they caught each other's eyes, something sparkled. Catharina knew it was unlikely to last, but she did not care. Tomorrow did not matter and felt so far away. Tonight, anything was possible.

She and Janus talked mostly about the war. Catharina did not normally like to, but she found it refreshing with someone she had not known then and who could not judge her. The six years of the Second World War were extraordinary in many ways. People did what they had to, to survive. Catharina allowed her thoughts to drift off and consider what her husband had done to her then, what he had done to both of them. It was the first time she had pictured him since leaving home and the light she presently enjoyed quickly turned to darkness. He was trying to score points, she thought bitterly. Anger and tears were building. She took a breath and drank some more wine. She looked at Janus, who returned to focus in front of her.

He was from Warsaw and had been a talented athlete in his youth. He had left school at sixteen, joined the army, and proudly fought in the Polish resistance. He had survived the Nazi occupation and joined the Russians when they liberated Warsaw, fighting alongside them all the way to Berlin. He was half-Jewish, but he had successfully hidden his identity, working as forced labour for the Germans during the war. Janus was a good worker and he did not trust anyone, the marriage of which had safely protected him. He had fought with his father when he was a child and he was glad to leave home.

Catharina hid her alarm when Janus said he did not know what had happened to his parents, his only immediate family 'thankfully', during the war.

But he knew going home would almost certainly have meant the death camps. He did finally return at the end of hostilities in the spring of 1945, but found another family living in their house. They became angry when he asked after the original occupants and said they knew nothing of them and that they had always lived there.

'That's awful,' said Catharina. 'How could they get away with it?'

'It was quite common,' explained Janus. 'People were suspicious of

Jewish homes and possessions before the war and they felt perfectly entitled to them after the Nazis shipped them to the ghettos. It was their inheritance.'

'That is terrible Janus. I'm so sorry,' said Catharina.

'Do not be,' he said.

Janus then revealed he was 36, which secretly stunned but thrilled Catharina, who had thought him to be ten years younger.

'If you thought the Germans were bad,' said Janus, returning to the war. 'The Russians were animals. They murdered, raped and burnt everything in their path on the way to Berlin. I knew it would be no better under them. The Russians said it was revenge for what the Germans did to their people, but it was not revenge. How do you say? They liked it. I managed to get to Berlin in 1945, in the Soviet sector at first. It was what I knew. But I escaped to the West through the subway and chose Munich. It was quite simple. Here, no one dares hate Jews for fear of being investigated as a war criminal. Before, people feared not hating Jews.'

'Yes,' said Catharina, half-laughing, which she immediately felt was grossly inappropriate, but she loved hearing him talk. 'That is a good way of putting it. I never knew anti-Semitism was still so strong in Europe. I suppose you don't hear it on the wireless in Germany, because we don't want to talk about it. Why would we? We hated the Jews more than anyone.'

'Shall we go?' asked Janus. 'I think the waitresses are keen to finish for the night.'

They were the only customers left in the café. Most of the candles on other tables had been blown out and with them, the magical intimacy of the evening was largely gone. It felt like time to go.

'Can I walk you home?' asked Catharina.

'Aren't I supposed to ask you that?'

The couple slowly walked the short distance back to Janus' flat on Georg-Elser-Platz. It only took them five minutes.

Catharina wished it could have been five hours. She did not want this evening to end. It was cold. The raincoat she had chosen for its lack of bulk was now proving too fragile against the fresh air. She wanted to grab Janus and huddle up against him while they walked, but she dared not.

Janus wanted to offer Catharina his jacket to comfort and warm her shoulders, but he too dared not. That would seem too forward, too presumptuous, he thought.

They stood outside the butcher's and the sight of something familiar killed some of the romance for Catharina. Tonight had been about being different. The meat looked strange hung up in the darkness behind the large glass front.

'It looks like an abattoir in there,' she said, using her cupped hands as blinkers against the street light to peer through the glass.

'I suppose it does,' said Janus.

'Would you like to meet again?' she asked. It was now or never, she thought.

'Yes, I would.'

'You know I am married.'

'I know you're married,' said Janus, smiling. 'Your wedding ring,' he added, pointing.

'Of course,' said Catharina, strangely relieved. She found herself looking uncomfortably at the floor for a third time this evening. She sensed Janus was close.

'Catharina,' he said.

She looked up and held his eyes in hers this time and the world around them fell away. This was the moment she had imagined.

Janus curved his hands around Catharina's petite waist. She put her arms around him and felt the power in his shoulders. Janus wasn't much bigger than her, but after the stories she had heard tonight, he was a fighter, a survivor.

She could not be sure how long the kiss lasted. Time drifted and she forgot where parts of her body ended and where parts of him began. They unlocked lips and Catharina felt embarrassed to have too much saliva slipping out of her mouth, like she had been greedily taking the opportunity to drink too much of him in. She smiled, glancing down like a teenager and waiting for him to say it was okay. Janus smiled back. He did not mind. He liked it. It only made her more real, more feminine. They embraced like they were about to part for a long time. She looked into Janus' eyes. They were so close it was a blur, but only more beautiful. She picked out individual eyelashes.

CHAPTER EIGHTEEN

It was Monday morning and Jozef did not feel great. He was trying to eat a deliberately plain breakfast of cereal and cold milk, but his temporary depression, after a weekend of heavy drinking, made eating difficult. He felt breathless and panicked. His sluggish mind anchored him down and he had already vowed several times this morning to not drink the next weekend, despite it being an entire week away. At this precise moment, he could not face another gloomy start beginning to a Monday.

Jozef had a lecture in just under an hour at 9am. The university dining hall was sparsely filled by only the most conscientious undergraduates like Jozef, who were not going to let a hectic weekend affect their attendance.

Others, including Pierre and Mathias, were not quite so scrupulous. Martyn was free until 11am and could afford to lie in a little longer. They had each pulled the covers over jetlagged heads and were hoping to sleep it off.

Experience had taught Jozef you only ever really felt better after facing up to the world. At least now he could sit alone with his thoughts. He could not have handled someone bleating in his ear, overcompensating for not feeling well by trying to talk their way out of it. Jozef wanted to quietly overcome his unease.

'In the late 1920s,' began the bearded professor, who Jozef had grown to quite like. 'Hitler visited a professional photographer's studio to have a set of portraits done. He wanted to show Germans how dynamic he was; he wanted to show them that he was a real revolutionary. In hindsight, given even Hitler's terrible heritage, he does look ridiculous.'

Muted laughter from the galleries could be heard as the professor clicked through a brief slideshow of portraits Hitler had had taken. He did look ridiculous, thought Jozef.

'Hitler developed a habit of holding people's gaze an unnaturally long time when they met. He wanted people to remember him; he wanted them to believe in his awe. Hitler was helped at this time by communism to the East and Russia. The German political and social elite backed Hitler not because they were so impressed by him, but because they were afraid of communism.'

Outside of lectures, Jozef really liked Pierre. He could not believe someone so cool wanted to socialise with him.

Pierre felt the same. He could not believe someone so together, so grounded wanted to spend time with him.

The pair of them were enjoying a quiet drink in a pub not far from campus. It was a Tuesday evening. They were both about a third of their way through a beer. Pierre lit a cigarette and, as he often did, inadvertently blew smoke up into his eyes, which made him squint fiercely. Jozef loved the look. He thought Pierre was uber fashionable. Pierre himself thought he was a mess and drowning in a degree in German literature which seemed increasingly beyond him. He could not discipline himself to hand in essays on time and on the odd occasion he did, he felt his hard work went unrewarded, which only spiralled him back down into depression, ensuring he would be late with his next piece. So the cycle had repeated itself in his first year.

Jozef believed everyone at university was more intelligent than him and was still to learn that the odd fierce opinion and constantly smoking cigarettes did not mean someone automatically had a spectacularly high IQ. He was still to miss a deadline in Berlin. He was usually early handing in his papers and had found the odd untidy professor did not want them so soon. It threw them. They wanted work handed in strictly on deadline – not before, not after. The day itself. Jozef could not help himself. He preferred to incur a little wrath for being a day early rather than suffer what he assumed would be terrible admonishment were he a moment late.

'How are your courses going?' Jozef asked, taking a mouthful of beer and enjoying early sparks of intoxication in his head.

'Okay. You?' Pierre said, conscientiously stubbing out his cigarette so Jozef did not have to inhale second-hand wisps whirling up from the ashtray separating them. Pierre appreciated Jozef was one of the few people he knew who did not smoke and did not like cigarettes, especially in midweek when there was no wild drunkenness to increase his tolerance.

'Fine, I guess,' said Jozef. 'I feel I should be doing more; I feel I should be doing better.'

'Jozef,' said Pierre. 'You're one of the hardest working people I know. You always get good marks for your papers and you're on course to get exemptions from every end of year exam. You'll be able to go home early while the rest of us are stuck here, sweating it out.'

'I guess,' said Jozef uncertainly. 'I'm not sure I want to go home.'

'Why not?'

'Are these two dead?' interrupted a round barmaid. She was holding the two empty glasses up to the light like she was checking for forged Deutsche Marks.

'Yes,' said Pierre.

The worn woman, with impossible breasts spilling out from a low-cut top, quickly placed two full glasses of beer in their place.

'Danke,' said Jozef, but the lady was already gone and sharing laughter with two men closer to her age nearby. One of them squeezed her bottom, which was bigger than the moon. Jozef gulped some beer queasily and tried to look away.

'Can I tell you something?' he asked his friend.

'Of course you can,' said Pierre, reaching a kind hand forward.

A man drinking and smoking religiously alone on a neighbouring table did not miss the moment.

'Puffs,' he said bitterly under drunken breath.

Neither Jozef nor Pierre heard him, which was good on either part.

'Promise me you won't tell anyone,' said Jozef, looking Pierre deliberately in the eye and raising the old drunk's suspicions further.

'I promise. I won't tell anyone. You can trust me.'

Jozef felt he could trust someone for the first time since Sebastian and then his parents had betrayed him. There had only been Michael left and Jozef was unsure if his childhood relationship with his father's friend was going to translate so easily into adulthood.

'I know I can,' he said.

Taking a deep breath, he said, 'I grew up an only child in Munich. My parents, I suppose, are working class. They both have their problems, but my relationship with both of them has been good. They told me something the night before we came to Berlin. They told me I wasn't their son by birth. They told me I was adopted.' Jozef finished and breathed deeply. He had tried to be as clinical and economical with the truth as he could. He did not want to add unnecessary emotion to his confession, because he was not sure it would have been either appropriate or truly reflective of his feelings. The truth was Jozef did not know yet what he felt.

'Blimey,' said Pierre. 'I thought I had problems. How old were you when they adopted you?'

'I don't know. I was too stunned to think to ask. The next day we came straight here and university was all I was trying to think about.'

'That's understandable. Do you know any more?'

'I don't know anything else. But I think I want to know now.'

CHAPTER NINETEEN

Gerhard and Catharina were having supper. Neither of them was saying much. Both, for once, were perfectly content. Gerhard was happy satisfying the huge hunger he felt after work and Catharina was quietly thrilled reliving her kiss with Janus. She had briefly seen him in the butcher's earlier this morning while shopping. The two of them had enjoyed sharing a momentary look and making teasing eyes. They did not feel alone anymore among the stress and drudgery of their daily lives. They had someone who understood how and what they were feeling; they had someone to look forward to. The transformation in Catharina's general mood was unbelievable. She could suffer Gerhard more; she could suffer chores more; she could suffer life more.

'Michael has invited both of us out for a dinner in the city,' Gerhard said without looking up from his newspaper. 'Next Thursday.'

Next Thursday? No. Next Thursday, Catharina thought. Janus.

'I have to sing, darling. We're really very busy at the moment with the choir. The conductor has big plans for us this year,' she explained as casually as she could.

'I know,' said Gerhard. 'But this sounds important. How often does Michael invite us out?'

Catharina started to resign herself to defeat and in her head agreed with her husband. Michael never invited both of them out together. She felt frustrated and low getting ready for bed that night. Reality had reminded her that any affair she was about to have – and how she craved it now – was not going to be as simple as she had naively begun to believe. She knew she had a safe hour before Gerhard would follow her up, so Catharina sat in front of her mirror and wrote to Janus.

Dear Janus,

I am afraid I will not be able to make our date next week. I have to go to dinner with my husband and the man who gave us our adopted son. I am sorry. I feel terrible. I will be at the café instead a day later, same time. If you can make it, it would be wonderful to see you. I have been thinking of you. Catharina x

That Thursday, Catharina dressed for dinner with Michael in the city with trepidation. She did not like Michael. She never really had. Her instincts had demanded that.

'Darling, are you nearly ready?' called Gerhard, who had been nearly ready for half an hour.

Catharina sensed panic in her husband's voice. He hated letting Michael down. She did not really know why. What did he feel he owed these people?

'Five minutes,' she shouted back downstairs.

Catharina sat at her mirror and looked at her make-up. She checked her hair and she checked the necklace she was wearing delicately around her neck. She was putting off going.

'It's now or never,' she said to herself, rising from her seat and collecting a shawl for warmth from the end of their double bed.

Gerhard was stood waiting for her at the bottom of the stairs. He had already had a drink.

Catharina could smell it on him, but more than that. She could feel it in his manner. She would forgive him for drinking excessively tonight. She frankly did not care if he made a fool of himself. Do your worst, she thought.

Gerhard was already in the driver's seat of their car when Catharina closed and locked the front door behind her. It was dark and cold and she felt naked in the night air. She could already feel Michael's unsolicited eyes admiring her shape. She tried to put it to the back of her mind and pulled the shawl protectively around her shoulders and chest. Dashing quickly in her best heels to the car, she opened the door and climbed in. Gerhard immediately ignited the engine and pulled out of their driveway, heading into the city.

'Catharina, Gerhard,' beamed Michael in the majestic ballroom hosting tonight's dinner.

Everyone was enjoying a drink, champagne exclusively, served by waiters and waitresses, before being called for dinner. Catharina and Gerhard were placed on a table for eight with Michael and five people they did not know.

'How are you both? Lovely to see you. Catharina, you are a vision. You have outdone yourself this evening.'

Catharina struggled to smile in return.

Michael found her extremely desirable, lusting from a distance after her delicate feet, slim legs and, despite her years, toned hips. Gerhard was oblivious to the tacit friction between his wife and the man who had given them their son. Michael was not about to miss the opportunity to kiss Catharina generously on both cheeks. He slipped his hands a little too low around Catharina's waist while doing so. Gerhard's focus was elsewhere – on where his next drink was coming from.

He spied a waitress and intercepted her. The waitress watched Gerhard approach before meeting him halfway with three glasses of champagne on her tray. Michael already had a glass and had declined another so soon. Gerhard was tempted to grab both of the other glasses greedily for himself after first handing one politely to Catharina, but even he drew the line at that, although perhaps he would have, he thought, if Michael had not been so close.

The ballroom was a loud hum of people and chatter and ceremony. Grand chandeliers hung decadently overhead and Gerhard felt uncomfortable – he needed more liquor – and above his station in such company. He had always had an acute sense of his own low social standing and hated moving much above or below that status. Catharina did not care for her surroundings this evening either. She could only think of Janus and the intimacy they had shared in the café.

Michael was thriving. He feasted on occasions like tonight. It made him feel privileged, important, a man to look out for and to talk about admiringly out of earshot. Michael's ego thrilled in the knowledge that people talked about him after he had left the room and had moved on to regale a neighbouring soiree. He daydreamed about it constantly. He had done so his whole life.

'I'll see you both at the table. Dinner will be called in ten minutes.

There is a table plan over there,' he said, motioning to a large, white sheet on the wall near a long bar, which stood empty.

'Ladies and gentlemen,' announced a grand voice and this evening's master of ceremony. 'Dinner will now be served. If you would like to make your way through to the dining hall, please.'

The sooner tonight is over, the better, thought Catharina, bracing herself.

Michael held out Catharina's chair when she and Gerhard reached their table in the impressive dining hall. There were two other places free on the large but busy round table.

'Danke, Michael,' Catharina said politely.

There were smiles from other faces sat anonymously around. Catharina could hardly stand Michael's nauseous show of servitude. She noticed no one else sympathised and she felt alone. Gerhard began pouring people wine happily from bottles left unopened on the table. She could see he was mildly drunk already. He would say more to these people tonight than he had to her in a month.

'Gerhard, Catharina,' said Michael, who had naturally taken it upon himself to host the table. 'This is Herr Tomas Klinker and his good wife Frau Katherine Klinker.'

'How do you do?' said Catharina.

'And this is Herr Johan Strudell.'

'Delighted, Frau Diederich,' said Johan, rising to his feet and delicately taking Catharina's right hand in his own and kissing the top of it.

Catharina felt like it was 1859 not 1959 and was even more out of place.

'How do you do, Herr Strudell?' she said, maintaining etiquette.

Michael was in heaven over dinner. He seduced the ladies and he entertained the gents. He seemed at first glance like a man for everyone, but Catharina knew who he really was. The conversation for a moment at their table was led by others, Michael quietly asked Catharina, 'How is your steak this evening?'

'Lovely.'

'Better than the meat you buy in town?'

'The meat is beautiful this evening,' said Catharina, lying.

She liked her steak pink but this was bloody and starting to make her senses turn. Gerhard was sat next to Catharina but out of immediate earshot. He was drunk and had his back turned, clumsily regaling other guests at their table. Their volume had momentarily increased through laughter. Michael seized upon the chance.

'I see you are particularly fond of your butcher on Georg-Elser-Platz.

How could tonight compare,' he paused, searching, relishing the right words. 'To that personal touch?'

Michael pulled himself away from Catharina's side and began smiling falsely again at the other guests at their table.

Catharina froze and her skin flushed hot. She struggled to breathe. She instinctively wanted to flee the scene, but felt trapped by this predator poised so close.

'Are you okay, darling?' said Gerhard, oblivious to the discreet exchange which had just shaken his wife.

'Yes, yes, fine,' said Catharina, hurriedly trying to deflect attention from herself. She felt everyone at the table was staring. 'I'm just going to use the restroom quickly. Excuse me.'

All the gents rose in archaic unison. Michael held his thick white napkin to his mouth, dabbing at traces of gravy around his lips which were not there. He was smiling.

Catharina rushed away and people assumed she was going to be sick, perhaps having childishly enjoyed rather too much champagne this evening. Her head was reeling. She felt the giant dining hall was on the Bismarck and had just struck an iceberg. Her world lurched, tipped on its side. Walking straight proved difficult. Her mind raced, and she could not collect her thoughts, strewn pitifully on the floor. What did Michael mean? What did he mean? How could he know? He could not possibly know. She had been so careful. Catharina thought she had been so careful.

CHAPTER TWENTY

Jozef was looking forward to his seminar with Professor Zielinski. He enjoyed them. The professor's relaxed, non-judgmental style had gently encouraged Jozef to open up over the course of the academic year. The delicate process was also helping Jozef slowly bloom in Berlin outside the classrooms and lecture theatres.

Everyone arrived on time today, which was a rarity. They sat snugly in a tight circle with the professor at its natural head. There were six undergraduates alongside Jozef – it was a full house.

The professor caught Jozef's eye. He knew he had to put him at ease if he were to talk today and not be dominated by more confident but perhaps less intelligent peers.

'In February 1933, Hitler first addressed the German nation after becoming chancellor. He made them wait. If Germans were waiting for key details of his new policy at home and abroad, they would be disappointed. Hitler never went into detail in his speeches, I would argue, because it was never there. Of course, Hitler had goals – target the Jews and anyone else he believed were his enemies at home – but he did not have a grand plan, mapped out meticulously before him.'

The professor continued, 'Hitler was arguably an old-fashioned opportunist. All he told the German people in February 1933 was "beware foreign help", planting the seed in people's minds that they should hold a very insular view of the world and a hostile outlook when they gazed beyond Germany's borders.'

The morning sun radiated brightly outside. The blinds were closed, but light still glinted kindly through, relaxing the space.

Only Jozef was taking notes, noted Professor Zielinski.

'In April 1933, a one-day boycott of Jewish shops and businesses was staged in Germany. If, in hindsight, it seems ominous to us, it didn't at the time. Hitler was clever. He distanced himself from controversy in his early days of power when his grip on it was still fragile. In June 1934, a powerful politician in Germany, Franz von Papen, spoke out against Hitler. Von Papen said, "Germany must not board a train into the unknown when no one knows when it will stop". No one listened.

'The German people weren't stupid, of course. They could see what was happening, but they felt only the ugly, unruly element within the Nazi party was to blame. They believed Hitler could not be blamed for every little thing that happened under his Chancellorship. He couldn't control everything, they said. He was still the way forward. After all, the economy was healthy now and Germany had order.'

'Why couldn't anyone see?' one female undergraduate asked earnestly. 'Hitler was a monster.'

'Power and fear,' said the girl who spoke too much immediately, making the professor wince quietly. 'People were scared of Hitler. What could they do against the Nazis? Speak out and you were killed.'

'Well,' said the professor, keen to quickly regain control of the room. 'That is true, but not the whole truth. Jozef, you have been quiet so far today. What do you think?' The professor did not like putting Jozef on the spot, but he felt he had to on occasion.

Jozef shuffled uneasily in his chair. His face flushed red and he felt the eyes of the room trained on him. He hated the sensation and wanted to run away. He gathered himself. I have to fight through this, he thought. 'We like to see the good in people, professor,' he began.

'Yes,' the professor encouraged.

It was the most intelligent thing anyone had said today.

'How could, why would Jews really believe the Nazis would kill them? If I was a Jew during the war, I don't think I would have believed it. Maybe people didn't until it was too late.'

Jozef felt the hot colour begin to drain from his cheeks. He had still been embarrassed and uncomfortable talking, but he had got through it and he had said what he had wanted to say – and under, for him at least, an intense spotlight. He did not thank the professor for that at this moment, but then he resented that reaction. Jozef wanted to like the professor.

'Excellent, Jozef,' congratulated Professor Zielinski, who felt his thoughts tip back in time to the war and Poland. 'Excellent. People want to see the good in people...'

It was 1942 and chillingly cold.

Men's breaths crystallised into icy fogs in front of their faces. Professor Zielinski had found that romantic once, but romance had long left Warsaw. The professor and three friends were huddled tightly around a large tin drum, which housed a small fire burning weakly within. It was the best they could do. Each man had a balaclava on and gloves of some kind – the professor's were fingerless. Why had he been so stupid in the rush of eviction to bring fingerless gloves? He hardly ever felt the tips of his fingers these days. Maybe the blood in his body would not bother travelling back down there soon. It would be afraid it was never coming back.

'Have you heard the rumours?' one man said.

'Yes, I've heard the rumours,' shrugged another.

'What rumours?' snapped the professor grumpily, reaching his hands as deep inside the drum as he dared.

'They are sending us to camps to be killed,' said the man, wrapping his arms around himself in an effort to keep warm.

'Who told you that?' growled the professor. 'Don't be so ridiculous.'

'They are packing people away on trains, in cattle cars. You are given no food or water. There is only a bucket for people to relieve themselves in and they are packed in so tight there is no room to sit – for days. Can you imagine? The smell?'

'Who told you that?' demanded the professor again, growing increasingly angry. His instincts warned him that there was worrying detail in the lie. A little boy, moth-eaten and starving, tugged at the professor's leg. He did not speak but simply pointed to his mouth.

'I haven't got anything child,' said the professor, peering down at him impatiently and turning away momentarily from the group.

The boy was filthy. His teeth were black and rotting, and his eyes were sinking back into his head. Death was starting to take hold. Hunger did not allow the boy to concede defeat easily and he pulled again at the professor's leg, harder this time.

'Get off me boy!' the professor shouted and kicked out a leg, flinging the child to the ground and into the gutter where human faeces were swimming. He felt a pang of humanity. 'I'm sorry. I'm sorry, my boy,' said the professor, reaching down to pick him up, but the boy beat him to it, readjusting his cap and scrambling to his feet before sprinting off.

'Forget him,' one of the men said and the professor turned back to the group.

'When you reach the camp, everyone is hauled off trains and marched straight inside. They tell everyone to strip and they give you a bar of soap. Then you are marched through to a large room and they slam the doors behind you.'

The professor jumped when the man accentuated the word 'slam' and was immediately embarrassed for doing so.

'Professor Zielinski?' the girl who spoke too much said again.

The professor looked up. Six young people – clean and innocent – were staring at him. They looked concerned. It was sunny and warm and there was no danger in the room.

'Miles away! My apologies,' he said, hoping his students would not see the uncertainty and fear in his features.

Five didn't. Jozef did.

'That is all today. Good seminar. Well done everyone. Jozef, do you have a moment?'

'Of course, professor.'

'Jozef, I've thought long and hard about this, but I feel the time is right.'

'The time is right for what?' Jozef asked.

'To show you something,' said the professor, unbuttoning the cuffs of the sleeves of his shirt. 'To show you this.'

A tattoo. Strange. Jozef had little experience of tattoos, but this was certainly not how he might have imagined one. He looked closer at it, curious. A small, inky row of numbers, fading on the inside of the professor's wrist: 82367.

'I was in Auschwitz.'

'The concentration camp?' said Jozef, unsure.

'Yes. But it was a death camp, Jozef. It was a death camp.'

'What was it like? How did you survive?' said Jozef, firing questions at Professor Zielinski like gun shots.

'Patience, patience,' said the professor, who believed he had been right to tell his student, but who had not talked about it with anyone but fellow survivors before and even then, he had been guarded about what he had revealed. This felt right. Nearly fifteen years had passed. How many more did he have left – five? Ten? Fifteen maximum.

He unbuttoned the top button of his shirt, loosened his bow tie and looked calmly into Jozef's eyes. The only other people to have looked at Jozef that intensely were his mother and Michael.

Jozef was listening.

'Jozef,' said the professor, lowering his gaze. 'You must promise, you must absolutely promise, that what is said in this room when only we are present remains in this room. These words are not for the outside world. The outside world is not ready for what I am about to tell you, not yet.'

'Of course,' said Jozef. 'You can trust me. Anyway, I have a secret I want to tell you.'

CHAPTER TWENTY-ONE

Catharina's mind was in disarray. She desperately wanted to see Janus, but now her motives were sharpened by last night's dinner and the menace which Michael had whispered in her ear. She had been so intoxicated by the situation that she could not recall what he had uttered precisely. She wished she could, so she could relay the information faithfully to Janus. He would know what to do. She trusted him. He had survived the Nazis and the Red Army. A brief affair with a married, middle-class woman hardly compared, she thought.

Her mind span off again in another direction, then back to last night and what specifically Michael had said. All she could remember was recoiling violently from the table to the ladies' restroom. She remembered that nauseous moment vividly. She came to her senses and realised the teaspoon she was about to place next to the kitchen sink, newly cleaned, was not clean at all. She had missed a tiny chunk of egg on its back. Gerhard must have left it there after breakfast.

Catharina slept deeply for more than an hour that afternoon. She often catnapped for ten minutes on the sofa, but she was rarely so exhausted in the day that she climbed back into bed, fully clothed for comfort. When she woke her head had finally stopped spinning. Sleep had drugged the dizzying sensation. She could think clearly again.

She stood in front of her mirror. She had wanted to wear her favourite dress again for her second date with Janus, but she felt she could not. She had to wear something different. That night was gone, she told herself. She could not recapture it. Things had changed. He might not even show. She ran her hands down the seams of her skirt. Her head was starting to whirl again. She had poured herself a small whisky and water to help calm the sensation. Gerhard's suspicions had been aroused, she felt.

'Why are you drinking?' he said, looking up from his newspaper. 'It's not like you.'

It's not like bloody you either, Catharina cursed sarcastically in her head. 'I just felt like a pinch of Dutch courage tonight,' she said. 'We have our final dress rehearsal for our summer concert.'

'You didn't have to start going to choir again on my account,' said Gerhard.

'I want to go,' said Catharina. 'Honestly. It is good for me.'

Catharina reached the door to the café and opened it. The establishment's quaint bell rang, announcing her uncertain arrival. Customers were sparse tonight and the waitresses were different from before.

'Table for one?' said one, approaching Catharina, who stood politely waiting just inside the door.

'A table for two, please,' answered Catharina, collecting herself. 'I hopefully have a guest, a gentleman, this evening.'

'Very well, madam,' said the waitress blankly, leading Catharina over to a free table. 'Anything to drink?' she asked as Catharina sat down.

'Yes, a glass of red wine, please,' she replied, taking off her coat and fixing her hair.

Catharina looked up at the café's clock after drinking half a glass of red wine rather quickly. She was fifteen minutes early – if Janus showed. She realised then her mind would only be calmed by his arrival or the realisation that he was not coming. She would have to sit and suffer until that truth.

'Oh, Catharina,' she whispered to herself.

The wine was heavenly and started to massage her conscience. Her pulse slowed and she sank into her seat, watching the fragile flicker of the candle dance in front of her.

Janus came. Catharina saw him arrive and captured his eye immediately. It was only seconds before the waitress approached and invited him to sit down. But those few moments were torture for Catharina. She wanted to rush over and grab him, hold him and ask him if everything was alright – ask him if he forgave her.

'I forgive you,' Janus said ten minutes later. 'You are married. I understand. It would be stupid of me not to.'

Catharina looked into his eyes and smiled before feeling uncomfortable again being so direct, so confident. She broke eye contact and began playing with the rest of her red wine.

'I was annoyed with you for five minutes maybe,' Janus said.

'Good,' said Catharina. 'I would have been annoyed with you for five days.'

Janus looked uncomfortable.

'I didn't mean that,' she said, hastily retracting her statement. But Catharina realised that was exactly what she had meant.

'I don't want to sit here tonight,' said Janus, finishing his wine. 'I hoped you would come and see my flat, above the shop. It is what I hoped we would do last night.'

Catharina wasn't sure what that meant. The proposition was both intoxicating and terrifying in the same instance. She ran her hands down her skirt beneath the table. Her aim this time was purely to iron out creases in her imagination. She did not think it had worked.

They strolled casually like in the movies down the streets back to Janus' flat. There were not many people around, which calmed Catharina. It felt right clasping Janus' strong arm and feeling his figure brush against hers. He moved his head down slightly and kissed her gently. There was magic in his touch. Catharina could not help herself blushing, even though it was cold. They reached his flat. Janus dug into his jacket pocket and produced a set of keys. He unlocked the front door to the premises, which were dark and asleep, and starkly different to the light and bustle of the working day.

Catharina followed Janus past the counter and into surprisingly cramped and underwhelming back quarters. The lights remained off. Janus turned left and found a flight of stairs in the corner of the room, leading up to his flat. There was another door at the top, which was closed. He unlocked the door. Catharina peered over his shoulder through the mystery and felt she was entering another world.

'This is it, I'm afraid,' Janus said from the far end of the flat.

He felt a long way away.

Catharina instantly clocked a tiny kitchen and toilet through the back of the bedsit where he stood. The rest of the space between them – Catharina had still not left the sanctity of the flat's doorway – housed a large double bed, wrapped in a wonderful wool rug. You could have flown on that rug, she thought, in your dreams when you were little. Catharina felt she could try. She was seventeen again, untouched and unsure.

There was a desk to Catharina's left and, the room's best feature, a large bay window. Janus paced over and pulled across the curtains quickly and easily. They were thin and only diluted the moonlight. The rest of the space was bare, bar a tiny, ragged wooden table which allowed a wireless to stand tipsily like a happy drunk. Janus turned it on and found some jazz. Catharina was in heaven.

'What do you think?' he said, for once on the back foot in their relationship.

Catharina found the change in dynamic between them sweet. 'I love it,' she said, walking over to him and kissing him deeply.

He had not been expecting that. He had anticipated having to make the first move.

The kiss was guiltier than either of their embraces before. Catharina felt the frame of Janus' torso closely, running her palms and fingers over the contours of his chest. Janus' hands moved to Catharina's hips, which made her flinch at first. They unlocked lips. She started to pull off his white shirt, which hid attractive skin, crisscrossed with scars and little pits, like a miniature battlefield all of its own.

Janus completed yanking his shirt over his head, which had proved awkward. Catharina had not given him time to unbutton it fully and they bumbled between them over to their right and the bed, like a fighter plane spinning out of control. They collapsed and continued kissing. Janus took over and flipped Catharina, who had been on top of him, onto her back. He turned her around so her back was exposed and vulnerable before him. She undid her blouse and pulled it off with Janus' help, revealing a small but pretty bra and the knee-length skirt she still had on below her tiny waist which Janus gripped and squeezed with his hands.

Catharina had forgotten who she was for a moment. She had become a different person, a different woman entirely. It was unreal to feel his touch and embrace, and his lips plotting seductively across her neck before passionately rediscovering hers. She had waited her whole life for this.

Janus unclipped her bra slowly, carefully. Catharina could hardly stand the excitement and felt she was about to explode. Where had her restraint of all those years gone – all those years working desperately to conjure up some feeling in the bedroom? Janus then slowed the pace of their desire down and began butterfly kissing her spine, from its top to its bottom. His kisses became harder, working their way down. Occasionally, he flicked his lips to the left or right, each kiss a tiny electric charge, tickling and seducing in the same gasp.

Later, Catharina's head lay luxuriously on Janus' chest.

He sat up in bed smoking a cigarette. She was blissfully happy, but she knew she had to leave in half an hour. Catharina wanted those minutes to drag stubbornly by for hours, but instead they seemed to be ticking away on fast forward.

'Are you happy?' she said, her left hand stroking his chest so softly her fingers barely touched.

'Are you?' he replied.

Catharina playfully hit him and briefly raised herself up to look at him. Her breasts, which had been hidden by the rug, tumbled out.

Janus could not help admiring them.

Catharina realised and smiled wryly before reaching back for cover. 'Are you happy?' she asked again more testingly.

'I do not think I was put on this earth to be happy,' he said.

'What kind of answer is that?'

The act of making love had broken down barriers between them like only it could. She could be more informal, more personal now. He was not yet fully reciprocating, although Catharina could not recall the last time she had climaxed quite so breathtakingly. Her whole world had shuddered.

'How can we be happy when there has been so much misery and so much death?'

'I suppose,' said Catharina, whose suburb of Munich had remained relatively untouched by the Allied bombardment, which had otherwise flattened Germany beyond normal comprehension. Germany had protected her for much of the war from the murderous whirlwind which had enveloped and continued to displace millions in Europe. Such remarkable fortune made her feel guilty suddenly.

CHAPTER TWENTY-TWO

'You don't have to tell me anything,' said Professor Zielinski. 'This is not how I imagined this working. It's not why I am telling you this. I want to tell someone I was in Auschwitz; I need to tell someone I was there – I survived,' said the professor.

'I think I know that, professor,' said Jozef, placing his briefcase back on the floor beside his chair. He had been holding it all this time as if he were about to get up and leave.

'You haven't got anything timetabled for the next hour?' asked the professor, more business-like again.

'I haven't got anything until 1pm this afternoon.'

The sun peered out from behind clouds and filtered into the room, catching Jozef's eyes and forcing him to try and move to avoid it.

The professor climbed out of his seat and reached for the blinds. He started talking. 'I shall begin now, at my own pace and from when I see fit. Interrupt whenever you want. You know I would want you to. I want to engage with you. This is not some form of therapy for me.'

'Okay,' said Jozef.

The sun became blanketed by cloud in the sky. Jozef could tell, because the tunnels of light in the room turned dim and grey.

'I was working at the university in Vienna when the Nazis annexed Austria in March 1938. Jews were hit hard straight away. I had a good wage and a beautiful apartment in the centre of the city. Life was wonderful. Suddenly I was more despicable than a dog. I was scrubbing the streets in a bow tie like a freak show. People stood and watched. I remember one well-dressed woman holding up a little girl above the crowds so she could see better. The girl was excited, happy.'

Jozef felt uncomfortable at the weight of such a confession. But he was spellbound, though slightly guilty for feeling so. He let the conflict in him subside.

Professor Zielinski was oblivious. Talking about this took too much effort and emotion. His eyes shifted, like they were rewinding and then fast forwarding through libraries of memories archived carefully in his head. 'Ten per cent of the people in Vienna, mainly in the north of the city, away from where I lived, were Jews. The other 90 per cent did not care about us after 1938. Many were glad to be rid of us. Austria held a national referendum on whether the country should be annexed by Germany. More than 99 per cent voted yes. I was in the less than one per cent.'

Jozef sat stiffly in his seat, perched precariously like he might fall forward at any moment. He could not bring himself to say anything. What could he say that would carry equal gravitas? The sun ducked in and out from behind clouds, constantly changing the light and mood in the space.

'Germany's and Austria's youth were taught to be prejudiced by the Nazis. They were told they were better than everyone else. The Hitler Youth sang songs, "If adults scold us, let them rant and scream". Hitler was telling the next generation to forget what their parents and their grandparents thought and believed, and to believe what he was telling them. They did. They thought we, Jews, were weak. Hitler told them to despise weakness. But we had to be stronger than anyone otherwise we would have died there and then, millions of us.'

'I find it fascinating to note that not everyone – enemies aside – even by 1938 was head over heels in love with Hitler,' the professor continued, taking the heat out of the exchange for a moment. 'The British prime minister, Neville Chamberlain, commented, after negotiating the German annexation of Czechoslovakia in the autumn, that Hitler was "the commonest little dog he'd ever seen".'

'Ha!' exclaimed Jozef and the professor was pleased with his response. He really was very fond of his student.

'In 1939 another general in the German army, Ludwig Beck, stood up against Hitler. War was inevitable now. Beck saw that and was against it and resigned. He could see Hitler was a psychopath and wrote, 'I warned and warned and at last I stood alone'.'

'Beck was not alone. But he was alone in being brave enough to stand against Hitler. Hitler's other generals felt it was madness to invade France in the West and "unworthy of a civilised nation" to slaughter Poles and Jews in the East. Why did they not all stand together against Hitler?' asked the professor rhetorically. 'Because they believed, probably correctly, that the army, soldiers themselves, was too loyal to Hitler and would never have followed them. So they did nothing.'

That evening, Michael telephoned Mathias' father for the latest on Jozef's movements at university.

'He is spending a lot of time with a professor, a Professor Zielinski I believe,' Mathias' father dutifully informed Michael.

'Zielinski,' Michael said playfully, whirling the word around like good wine. He instinctively knew the name was Polish and most probably Jewish. 'Anything else?'

'Not an awful lot, to be honest,' said Mathias' father, holding the receiver to his right ear.

'That is fine,' said Michael, who was still processing the name Zielinski. 'Keep at it,' he added.

'Of course, of course. As soon as I hear anything you will be the first to know.'

'Very good.'

'Auf Wiedersehen,' said Mathias' father, but the line was dead by the time his words came out.

CHAPTER TWENTY-THREE

Catharina and Gerhard entered a period of real happiness. Catharina had Janus to look forward to every midweek and Gerhard had alcohol. Their upbeat moods meant they had not got on so well in years, not since Jozef was small. Gerhard's demeanour towards his wife improved because he felt she had given up monitoring his drinking and Catharina's behaviour improved towards her husband because as a consequence he had lost his tense edge. He was happy. She was happy.

That evening Michael visited Gerhard, knowing Catharina was at choir practice but most likely doing anything but singing. He did not really care. She could have her fun. Catharina was not a priority at present and could wait. Experience told Michael to employ it wisely if you enjoyed leverage over someone, and to never rush into blackmail.

Gerhard had quietly contemplated asking Michael something for weeks. He picked both his whisky glass and himself up from his chair. He wanted to stand over Michael. He wanted to feel in charge. This should be good, Michael thought.

'Is there a chance Jozef's birth parents will want a relationship with Jozef now or in the future?' Gerhard said, downing the rest of his whisky. He had gulped too hard and the strong liquor stung the back of his throat. He felt a failure already.

'I suppose there is always a chance,' Michael said slowly. 'You do not need to concern yourself with that. That is not your business.'

'Not my business!' Gerhard snapped. 'He's my son – our son. Catharina

would never get over losing him. Not now. Not after what happened.'
Happiness had imbued Gerhard with confidence.

'That was your choice.'

'You bastard,' said Gerhard. 'That was *your* choice.'

Michael smiled with menace almost and Gerhard felt he had
overstepped the mark, but he was committed now. He was afraid.

'If I am not welcome this evening,' said Michael, remaining calm, 'I will
take my leave. We will forget this little outburst Gerhard. I will forgive it.'

Gerhard was not sure he did. Gerhard did not think Michael forgave
anything. How could he, after all he had done?

Meanwhile, Catharina never believed sex with Janus could actually get
better. But it did. It got better. She created increasingly more elaborate
reasons why she would not be home. She shortened the gaps between their
dates and began seeing Janus on Saturdays afternoons, only returning home
to her husband in the evening after hours of heavenly, luxurious love-
making. She learnt to know where and how Janus liked to be kissed and
teased; she learnt to love the battered ugliness of his feet, which she had
initially disliked. The funny shape of his toes had been off-putting and she
had almost tried to hide from them the first couple of times they made love.
And she learnt to love the taste of him. She had never really liked that taste
before, but now she revelled in it.

It was 2pm, Saturday. Hours left. Catharina secretly rejoiced when she
noticed the time and it was firmly on her side. Sunlight was flooding over
their skin, sprawled on his bed. The butcher's opened only in the morning
on Saturdays, closing at 12noon sharp. Janus had the afternoon off and
Catharina and he had learnt to take full advantage. Janus would lock up
and promptly go out shopping for two bottles of white wine. He would
carry them both home, one in each hand, wrapped in crate paper. He
preferred red, if he was being truthful, but Catharina found it too rich in
the daytime. He did not mind.

He wanted to please her. He had not wanted to truly please a woman
since before the war – another lifetime. He felt protective of Catharina and
liked it. It gave him purpose and confidence and something else he could
not quite pin down. Maybe it was love, maybe it was happiness, though he
had once given up on both. He treated both emotions like a reformed
alcoholic treated drink – a foe not to be fooled with for fear of following a
path he knew too well where it ended.

The sky curving overhead was flatly grey, yet he saw beauty in it now when he went out to purchase wine for Catharina. He saw beauty in most things since the start of their affair.

Twenty expert paces behind, Michael was following. He had fixed his black gloves while he walked, so they helped protect his sleeves from unwelcome chills. He had planned his trip out to this part of town. Only an old drunk would buy two bottles of wine for himself, thought Michael, gazing up the pavement. And they were two decent bottles. A heavy drinker would surely adopt a more pragmatic, economical approach.

Janus reached his flat. Catharina was stood waiting as discreetly as she could. Janus smiled at her from a distance. She returned the compliment and undid her head scarf, allowing her hair to fall out into the wind and cold. She did not mind anymore. She liked the liberation. Looking around, she kissed Janus quickly. He wanted to wait until they were inside, but he smiled nonetheless. She took both bottles from him as he unlocked the door.

CHAPTER TWENTY-FOUR

'Professor, the day before I came to Berlin,' Jozef said after their seminar. 'My parents revealed something to me. They revealed that I was adopted. They are not my real parents.'

Professor Zielinski nodded kindly. He was not giving much away. He had not been sure what to expect from Jozef's confession, but whatever it was he certainly did not want to make the exchange more emotional than it had to be. He was keen to retain a degree of professionalism in the room.

'I think I want to know who my real parents are. I want to know who I am, but I don't know where to start.'

'I have a few ideas,' said the professor. 'Would you like some coffee?' He poured himself a cup.

'No, thank you. I don't drink coffee. My mother used to try and make me drink a little when I was a child, but I always cried. I didn't like how it scolded my mouth, so she gave up.'

The professor nodded, but he was only half listening if he was being honest. His craving for caffeine had temporarily taken hold. 'I could bathe in it if allowed,' he confided longingly and Jozef smiled. 'I can help you,' the professor said between sips. 'I can help you find your birth parents. The best place to start would be the central records office in Berlin. There is more information there than people know.'

'Can I ask about your tattoo?' said Jozef.

The professor felt too happy to launch into that subject. What was his tattoo really, he thought?

Jozef had taken the chance to drink from a cup of water placed carefully on the floor beside his chair. It was small, but twinkled with fragments of sunlight trapped in the glass.

'Did you know Jozef that the human lips become stretched in the final stages of starvation? It is called "the hungry grin".'

Jozef shook his head.

'Afterwards comes diarrhoea. Finally, a bitter taste in your mouth – like the body is poisoning itself. I thought it was telling me it wanted to leave, but my mind wanted me to stay. What can you tell me about your parents Jozef, the people who adopted you?'

Jozef liked that the professor used the word 'people'. The aloofness was appropriate. It made it easier for him to answer.

'Their names are Gerhard and Catharina Diederich. They live in central Munich and have done their whole lives I think,' said Jozef, who could not help noticing the professor's hair was particularly wild today. 'My mother, Catharina has always lived in Munich. My father may have moved about a bit but he settled after meeting my mother, which would have been close to 1930. I am 19 tomorrow, so I was born March 3, 1941.'

'Good, that is good,' the professor encouraged him, taking stock and drinking more coffee. 'And happy birthday for tomorrow. But you do not know what your surname is by birth? Or even if Jozef is your real name?'

'No, no, I don't,' said Jozef, shaking his head and finding that difficult – not knowing if Jozef was his real name.

'I suppose we also do not know for sure whether that birthdate is correct. We will have to presume it is.'

Jozef's eyes blew up. Sun gushed in from outside and he instinctively used his hands to protect his face from the glare.

'Let me get those blinds,' said the professor, annoyed the sun had interrupted their conversation. He knew this could not be easy. It had never occurred to Jozef before that March 3 was not his true birthday and that in fact he may have been in the wrong age group in education all his young life.

'I know this must be difficult Jozef. But we will get there.' The professor crouched forward onto the edge of his seat and clasped Jozef's hand in between his own. The man's hands were worn and creased like old newspaper. The professor patted Jozef's hand then let it go. 'We will go the central records office in Berlin. How are you fixed on Wednesday afternoon?'

That evening in Munich, Gerhard poured himself and Michael two large whiskies from the Diederich's drinks cabinet. Out of the corner of his eye,

Gerhard noticed Michael's legs were crossed and that one foot was swinging gaily, and rather annoyingly, in the air. Gerhard swallowed his anger, turned and handed Michael their most expensive glass.

'Thank you,' he said. 'Please, sit. Now, Gerhard, did you know Catharina was having an affair?'

Gerhard stopped. Not a lot got in the way when he was about to enjoy a first drink of the evening. But this did. His eyes dared not move for a moment.

'Yes,' continued Michael calmly. 'I don't know exactly who with, but I'm sure I can find out. No trouble.'

'You must be mistaken,' said Gerhard, returning to the conversation and drinking deeply from his glass.

'No. No mistake,' said Michael almost cheerily. 'I don't think Catharina's been very committed to the Munich ladies' choir lately, if you will.'

This added piece of information winded Gerhard. He had to lean forward in his chair to ease the discomfort. Michael smiled again.

It was Friday night and Gerhard and Catharina were eating a modest supper of kippers and boiled potatoes. It was perfectly pleasant but perfectly plain.

'Are you looking forward to your concert tomorrow?' Gerhard asked knowingly, guiltily. He felt uncomfortable and still could not believe it. Should he just come straight out with it? No. That did not feel right either.

'Very much,' said Catharina, eating a potato from her fork. 'I've been looking forward to it all week. I hope my practising in the bathroom hasn't bothered you too much!'

Catharina began to laugh, but stopped abruptly when her husband did not even smile in return. Unease.

'Is everything okay, darling?'

'Yes, yes, fine,' he stuttered automatically.

But Catharina sensed something was badly wrong. It was probably just a long week at work spilling over, she hoped, before thinking about what she was going to wear tomorrow. She was going to surprise Janus with new silk underwear. It had cost her the earth, but she was sure he would like it. She knew it flattered her figure and she began to feel aroused.

Gerhard was quietly going crazy across from her at the table. He was helpless before maddening thoughts of another man kissing her, touching her, *feeling* her. The stranger would not release hold of her in his imagination. Gerhard was willing him to. Fury was flooding his head and

Gerhard quickly needed to release the pressure otherwise he thought he might explode.

He stood up, paced around the room and tried to breathe.

Catharina knew now something serious was wrong. Breathe Gerhard, he told himself and he felt a little temperature drain from his mind.

'Darling, what's wrong?' asked Catharina.

'Nothing, nothing,' he said without thinking. 'There is a lot going on at work at the moment, that's all. I didn't get to where I wanted to today. I'll get stuck back into it on Monday.'

Catharina nodded happily. She had thought as much.

Gerhard had stopped moving, but he was still pacing frantically up and down, up and down in his head. The speed was increasing and he felt his heart burn. He reached for the door to the drinks cabinet, but then he stopped himself. Even a drink did not appeal. I'll follow her, he thought. Yes! I'll follow her. Gerhard was calm by the time he reached the bottom of his first glass of whisky half an hour later. He had a plan. He had a plan.

Next week soon arrived.

'Auf Wiedersehen, darling. Have a good time singing,' said Gerhard.

'Danke. I will,' said Catharina, closing the front door behind her.

Gerhard sprang up from his position at the dining room table. He had been pretending to read his newspaper for a small lifetime while his wife got ready to leave. He had not followed Catharina on Saturday. A hangover had dulled his desire and he had decided to leave it until the following midweek.

Gerhard already had his shoes on. He wriggled his arms into his jacket and checked he had his keys in his pocket, as he always had. Gerhard was nothing but a creature of habit. He closed the door quickly behind him but failed to check it was locked, which was healthy for him. He had paranoid compulsions which exhausted his days and his limited patience. He peered forward and made out Catharina a few hundred yards down the road. He feared he was losing her, but his instincts reminded him it was wise to hang back. Where on earth was she going? he thought. This was not the way to choir practice.

Gerhard watched his wife, a stranger now, buying a beautiful bouquet of flowers.

She was happy, happy in a way that he could not recall clearly. He was finding it difficult to witness what he was discovering and seeing what he had missed all these years. He stood discreetly across the street. Catharina walked out from the florists with her flowers, inhaling deep gulps of fragrance as she went. She was dressed smartly, attractively.

A man asked her what time it was. She looked at her wristwatch, slighter than her delicate wrists Gerhard had always loved. They felt so soft, so fragile, like he had to carefully cradle them for fear of breaking one by accident. Catharina told the man the time before sharing a joke. He laughed and tipped his hat to her.

Gerhard was losing her. He quickened his stride to keep pace, bustling his way past two women with large pushchairs dominating the pavement. There was no way past on the outside.

'How rude,' remarked one lady after Gerhard had finally barged past.

He thought about shooting words back in retort before glaring ill-temperedly in her direction instead.

Catharina stopped outside the butcher's.

It was closed, Gerhard saw, which he thought strange for a busy Saturday in Munich, but then again, he had no idea of the shopping habits of the city's inhabitants and shopkeepers. He could not remember ever going food shopping. What is she doing? he thought, annoyed. He was struggling to maintain his cover and was irritated his mind was running free from him. It was easier for his nerves if he moved while his mind raced. Then, a man, younger than Gerhard. Catharina held up the flowers to him. He half acknowledged her. She ran the last few paces and kissed him warmly on the cheek. The man seemed embarrassed and began to unlock the door. Catharina's hand rested intimately on the small of the man's back before she followed him inside.

Gerhard was crushed across the street. He felt queasy. His body was tingling with thousands of beads of sweat, scuttling across his skin like insects. They tortured him until he felt drunk, then sick on emotion. His mind retreated inside his head until he could only hear the people close to him gossiping. He was panicking and alone. Catharina had left him all alone.

CHAPTER TWENTY-FIVE

Jozef and Professor Zielinski were walking to the central records office in Berlin. They had caught the train and now faced a five-minute journey on foot. It felt peculiar, thought Jozef, to be with the professor like this outside campus and not strictly on university business. His search for his birth parents was beginning to demystify the professor. The layers were falling off him. It was both endearing and sobering in the same instance. The professor was not an untouchable institution in Jozef's eyes anymore. He was human and fallible like everyone else.

'Tell me more about the Nazis and their policies towards Jews,' said Jozef.

It was a good day, blue. There was no rush to reach the records office. It would be pleasant to while away the time and reintroduce something of a student-professor relationship to the dynamic.

'Yes, yes, of course,' said the professor, flanking Jozef. 'After annexing Austria, the Nazis put up loudspeakers all over the city. Hitler's speeches would play for hours and hours. At first you listened, but then it just became background noise. It was harder for us Jews. We knew Hitler's words carried greater significance. Hitler made no secret of his hatred for us.'

'There were pictures, pictures all over Vienna,' he continued. 'In them Jews were portrayed as monkeys and animals. We weren't people anymore. In the Jewish ghetto in Warsaw, where I ended up by 1942, conditions were terrible – ten to a room. There was a family in the room where I was placed – thankfully I had no family. I was alone. It was better that way, easier.'

'There was a couple who had two sons. One was crippled. He had rickets as a child, his mother told me. The illness had left him with a limp on his left side and he struggled to walk far. There was a hospital in the ghetto and the Jewish police, helping keep order for the Nazis, told the parents to send him there. The parents thought it was a good idea and that he would be safe. But the boy knew, I think.'

Jozef did not say anything. He thought it best to simply listen.

'When the policeman came to take him away the boy gave his mother his warm winter coat. It was a beautiful coat with a fur lining. His mother insisted he keep it, but he said, 'Mother, give it to someone who needs it. I don't need it anymore. It will be warm in the hospital'. He was twelve. The parents were deported the following spring. The other boy got a job, a good one, in an armament factory outside the ghetto. I don't know what happened to him.'

The professor realised where they were. 'Here we are, Jozef,' he said, geeing himself back up. That was enough sorrow for one day.

They stood on the grand steps outside the central records office. Jozef was wary of what lay undisturbed inside.

It proved a fruitless first trip. Afterwards, they had coffee and sandwiches nearby, resting tired feet and minds.

'Do not worry, I will put my thinking cap on,' said the professor, seeing Jozef was downbeat and disappointed. 'These things take time.'

'Tell me more about the camps,' Jozef said, trying to buck himself back up and refusing to wait for the ill feeling to subside naturally.

'Yes, yes, of course,' said the professor, who would rather not have turned the conversation there quite at this moment, but was glad to do something and, anyway, he had started this crusade, not Jozef. He could not abandon it now. 'What I am about to tell you is not easy. Camp survivors are not speaking about their experiences yet. I am of the opinion that one day they will and then we can all learn from them what really happened, and warn against anything like that ever happening again.

'When groups in society believe they are better and more valuable than others, a human disaster can occur. The Nazis told everyone Jews were not worthy of life like Aryan Germans. Everything I have told you and everything you have learnt until now has been worthwhile and of interest, but this is what really happened.'

The professor finished his coffee and braced himself. 'My greatest fear,' he began, 'is that once I and other survivors are all gone there will be no one left to tell people what happened – what really happened.'

There was so much life and energy surrounding them, Jozef observed who sat across from the professor in the café. The sun was threatening to set for the evening, but was still shining. It was strange to listen to the professor's terrible truths in such a setting.

'The first thing we went through was simply getting to the camps,' said the professor, careful to not let his words travel to another table.

A pretty waitress hovered over them and offered them more coffee.

The professor politely declined and continued speaking when they were safely alone again. 'We were crowded in like cattle on trains. There was no light, no food, no water, no toilet and no ventilation. I felt ashamed. How can a man hope other men die simply so he can have room to sit? That is what I felt. The Nazis dehumanised us. We were worse than animals. You became selfish. You did not care about anyone else. You really only cared about yourself.'

'That is not shame, professor, that is honesty,' said Jozef, feeling it was a good time to interrupt. 'I admire honesty.'

'Thank you Jozef,' said the professor. 'Shall we walk? It is getting cooler. We should get moving.'

The professor and Jozef walked slowly through the streets of Berlin peculiarly like young lovers, uncertain of one another but hoping one day to find happiness standing next to them.

'I would like to keep going,' said the professor and Jozef nodded.

Dusk was quickly turning to dark and street lights flickered into life. The university campus was not far.

'Something always struck me about the guards at the camps. The women guards were worst. Of course I had little experience of them, because they took care of the female inmates, and men and women were strictly separated upon arrival. But I remember one female SS guard with these eyes. I have never seen such hateful eyes. Where did they get women who hated so much? And for what?'

'What was it like when you first arrived?' asked Jozef, turning up the collar on his jacket to keep out the cold.

The professor had come well prepared and was now enjoying the warmth of thick gloves from his coat pocket. He clapped his hands together for extra heat while they walked. 'I spent time in another camp before I arrived at Auschwitz. It was chaos when we reached Auschwitz. You felt you had arrived at the gates of hell. God had long left. We got off the cattle train and stood on the platform. Waiting for us were Jozef Mengele and his cronies, dressed like peacocks in their Nazi uniforms.'

The professor's Polish thickened his German with feeling. He slowed and Jozef felt the cold. He tried to turn up the collar on his jacket further, but it did not reach higher around his neck.

'Mengele was flicking his finger,' described the professor. 'If he flicked it to the left, you were going straight to the crematorium. If he flicked it to the right you were going to the camp. Of course, we did not know in that moment.'

'There were SS troops with dogs and sticks and rifles. All these people going left were cripples, old people, children, babies and mothers holding babies. Troops told mothers to go right and drop the babies. But what mother would do that? They tried to rip the babies from the mothers' arms. If they couldn't, they shot the mother or shot the baby.'

The professor paused, thinking. 'I will never understand how a person can kill babies and then sit down at night and have dinner with a wife and children and listen to music.'

'We are back,' said Jozef.

'So we are,' noted the professor, gazing up to his right and the university lecture block towering across the street.

The professor started to feel the night in his bones. 'It has been quite a day. We will get there,' he said.

Jozef stood and watched him walk inside, up to his office for maybe something stronger than coffee.

'Jozef,' called the professor from the door. He waited until he had established eye contact from across the street. 'Danke.'

Jozef smiled as warmly as he could.

CHAPTER TWENTY-SIX

Gerhard was drinking whisky with Michael in his front room. Catharina was with *him*. The idea made Gerhard more intoxicated than the liquor. Relations between Michael and Gerhard had dipped lately and they both felt it in the space they now uneasily shared.

'I followed Catharina last Saturday,' said Gerhard. 'She is seeing a younger man. He lives above the butcher's on Georg-Elser-Platz.'

Michael said nothing and simply listened to his companion's confession. The clock on the mantelpiece sounded 9pm. Its cheap chimes were as uncomfortable as they both felt. Gerhard began to sob, but Michael could not deal with that. He thought it pathetic, particularly in a man.

'I could ask this Janus to move on,' said Michael. 'I am sure he would listen.'

'I never said his name,' said Gerhard, looking up from his pity. 'How do you know his name?'

Michael tried to paper over his error. 'It is my job to know these things,' he said. 'You should know that.'

Gerhard was tearful and too drunk to argue. He was also preoccupied with Michael's offer. His emotion turned to thoughts of revenge, which appealed to him. He wanted to hurt Catharina, hurt her like she had hurt him. It was tempting to ask Michael to make her leave Munich, but perhaps the best revenge would be to deprive her of this man.

'How can you be sure you can do it?' Gerhard asked Michael, who was enjoying his whisky and glad his verbal slip had not been analysed more deeply.

'I think you know what I am capable of. If you really do not, then know I am capable of this.'

'I don't want him hurt. Just away from here, away from Munich and out of our lives. For good.'

'I understand perfectly,' said Michael. 'There is something I now want from you. I want a new life for Jozef after he graduates. And I don't want you or Catharina to fight me on this when the time comes. I want you to support me when I put it to him.'

'A new life? What do you mean? I am sure Jozef will begin building a new life for himself after he leaves Berlin, but where that may be I do not know. I do not see it being here in Munich. Catharina maybe hopes it will be, but I am realistic enough to realise it won't.'

'I am talking about something a little more dramatic than another city. I am talking about another country, another continent – South America.'

'South America! We would never see him. Why South America?'

'His father has allies, powerful allies there. It could be the start of something, something important, something big for Jozef and for us. You know South America is the last haven we have?'

'I had heard of former Party members escaping there,' said Gerhard, pouring two more glasses of whisky.

Michael reached his right hand forward to lift his drink off the table. He opened his hand to signal his glass was full enough. 'Hitler had the vision for a thousand-year Reich, but not the mentality, the patience, the selflessness and the true outlook to realise it,' said Michael with alarming candour. 'Hitler tried to take over Europe in ten years. Suicide. But he was right when he said one thing, "We can be happy that the future belongs entirely to us".'

'You're insane,' said Gerhard.

'Quite sane,' said Michael before his tone cooled and darkened. 'Look,' he continued. 'Do you want that whore of a wife of yours to suffer or not? You danced with the devil quite happily before.'

'Catharina,' said Gerhard after supper the following evening. He hardly ever used her name. 'I know you are having an affair. I forgive you, but I am asking you to stop. I am asking you to end it.'

The words dropped like atomic bombs in the silence, mushrooming nightmarishly in Catharina's alarmed mind. She had been in the middle of scraping leftovers from their plates before carrying them through to the kitchen. She was desperately clinging on to them, head bowed. It was Saturday tomorrow.

Catharina had no idea what to say. She foolishly had not fully considered Gerhard unearthing her affair with Janus. She had not given him enough credit and she had stupidly discarded Michael's warning at dinner that evening in the city. Michael, she thought. Catharina picked up the plates and carefully made her way through to the kitchen. She was grateful to have a reason.

'Having an affair?' she then offered weakly. 'Gerhard, don't be ridiculous. Who told you I was having an affair?'

She reached the kitchen sink and stood absolutely still, awaiting her husband's response. Please God, she prayed, looking up for the first time since Gerhard had spoken.

'Catharina,' said Gerhard, using her name again. 'I saw you. I saw you outside the butcher's on Georg-Elser-Platz.'

Oh no. Oh no, she thought. She rushed back to their dining room, trying to half laugh off the accusation. The truth was she had never really experienced remorse for her actions.

'Darling,' she said. 'I should have told you, I know. I never should have done it. I have struggled since Jozef left.'

Gerhard knew that, but the pair of them had never sat down and properly discussed how displaced she felt. He could hardly take the moral high ground now. He would have only told her not to be so stupid had she tried to talk about it.

'How many times?' he asked.

Catharina sensed an edge in his voice. 'It's only been a few,' she said. 'We didn't do anything – just meet.'

'I saw you kiss. You have kissed,' said Gerhard.

'Yes, we have kissed,' Catharina immediately conceded. 'But nothing more, I promise you, darling.'

She was lying. They had had sex every time they had met since the second date. How many had there been since? Catharina had lost count.

'It has to stop,' said Gerhard, rising from his seat and reaching first for whisky and then a glass.

It can't stop, Catharina thought.

Early Saturday afternoon came.

'Gerhard knows,' Catharina said, lying naked with her head resting on Janus' midriff.

She had not gone to see Janus that Thursday for fear of exposing her affair further. She was desperate to protect her lover, but she was equally desperate to see him. The two emotions were irreconcilable.

114

'Someone told him,' she continued. 'They must have followed me one day.'

'It was inevitable,' Janus replied. 'Nothing good lasts forever.'

That was not what she wanted to hear. Catharina wanted comforting; she wanted more – not acceptance or philosophy. She thought she was special. Catharina reached for the sheets and pulled them over her exposed frame. She did not want Janus seeing her suddenly.

'What should we do?' she asked.

'I want you to do what you want to do.'

'I want you to tell me what to do,' said Catharina, turning around and looking up at his face.

'I want to see you,' Janus finally replied. 'I want us to see each other.'

Catharina bowed her head to hide her smile. This was what she had wanted to hear. She would have to go soon, but at least she would leave with hope in her heart.

'I like you, Catharina, I like you a lot,' said Janus, stroking her hair, which tickled and caused her to flinch.

'I like you too,' she said, rising up out of bed and exposing the back of her body.

Janus loved her round bottom and ached at its beauty.

Catharina quickly tried to cover herself, feeling far too vulnerable.

Janus saw her discomfort and reached for her, so she could not easily dress.

'Stop it,' she said, smiling.

'You are beautiful.'

Catharina was still uneasy accepting such compliments, even from someone she was now so intimate with. She felt the devil was trying to trick her.

'Janus, *you* are beautiful,' she said in her way of saying thank you. She turned around and rewarded him with the full sight of her and leaned in for a deep kiss, holding her frame up with her arms, so he could do what he wanted with the rest of her. She found that position most arousing when they made love.

'We cannot see each other on Thursdays anymore,' she said.

'I understand.'

'Can you get time off in the day during the week?'

'I can see if I can have a different afternoon off, but I would have to swap it for Saturday and make up the time. I will try.'

'Okay, good. Try,' said Catharina, pulling tights up her legs and preparing herself for her husband again.

'We have been happy, Catharina,' said Janus, still undressed and with only a sheet loosely covering him.

Catharina did not like the finality, the fatalism of his last statement. 'We *are* happy,' she said defiantly.

CHAPTER TWENTY-SEVEN

Jozef wanted to visit the central records office in Berlin alone. It was late but he knew it did not close until 10pm. He had had an idea.

'Guten Abend,' he said to the smart lady policing the front desk.

'Guten Abend. How may I help?'

'Do you keep records of children born in other parts of Germany, in Munich particularly?'

'We do. You would normally need to go to the family records centre,' said the lady. 'But it is closed from 6pm. I can bring the files up for you to look at. You will have to sign for them. Do you have identification?'

'Yes,' said Jozef, digging in his pockets for his university papers. 'My name is Jozef Diederich. I am an undergraduate at the university.'

The lady scanned Jozef's papers and handed them back to him. 'What years would you like to look at, Herr Diederich?'

'1935 to 1945,' he answered and waited while the lady left the front desk and made her way down to where the relevant records were kept.

She sighed as she went. She was clearly not thrilled to be working this evening.

Jozef looked about himself. He was in a cavernous corridor with double doors to large rooms in front of him. Behind his back, the building seemed closed off to the public. It was dark and quiet and alien from the daytime bustle of his last visit with Professor Zielinski. He could have done with some company, he thought as he sat down and waited. The lady reappeared pushing a cart carrying huge tomes of information. Jozef felt hopeless when he witnessed the magnitude of the task.

'Herr Diederich, here are the birth records for Munich, 1935-1945,' the lady announced. 'Would you like to come through to a table in the main library where you can view them?'

'Yes, yes, thank you,' said Jozef, dutifully following the lady.

He saw a security guard return to his post near the main entrance and immediately felt better for seeing another person. The guard was reading a newspaper, *Süddeutsche Zeitung*. Jozef recognised it because it was the one his father read.

He felt overwhelmed when the lady left him alone with the intimidating slabs of records. He at least had a large table to himself inviting him to begin his search. Half an hour went by. Nothing. The fact that nobody else was reading records this evening was hardly helping his motivation. Jozef's will was waning.

The lighting was poor in the library. Jozef had a spotlight on his table, but it was weak in all this space. He had to move the heavy volumes close to it to scrutinise their secrets. A figure, or so he envisioned, moved outside his line of vision. He exercised his shoulders to try and shake off the concern. The moonlight, slanting in from imperious glass windows, must have been playing tricks.

Jozef reached the volume containing the records of births in Munich in 1941. He drank from a glass of water he had received from the lady at the front desk to revive his senses and started wading through the pages to March 3, his birthdate. More pages. He scanned down the Ds: Daecher. Decher. Diederich - here they were - running his finger down the names. Johan, Johan, Johan, another Johan. Jozef. Jozef. His heart froze.

'Diederich, Jozef. Born 5.30pm, March 3, 1941. Central Munich Hospital. Parents Gerhard and Catharina...'

More movement, definitely, at two o'clock. Someone was there. Was someone there? Jozef flushed with heat and started to panic. He slammed shut the books and heaved them into an uneasy topple back on the cart. He pushed the heavy contraption in front of him as quickly as he could without careering out of control. The safety of the double doors lay ahead, like a sanctuary begging to be reached, opening out into the main lobby and people, life. Jozef span his head around. He almost did not want to risk it, but his instincts forced him. He saw it again, he thought.

He startled like a horse and abandoned the cart of books, dashing the last few yards to the double doors and barrelling through them, and stinging his shoulder painfully in the process. He saw the lady at the front desk peer curiously down her glasses at him. He was panting. Jozef immediately felt better, safe in the presence of the clerk. His heart was still pounding.

'The books are on the cart by the door,' said Jozef, gasping slightly. 'I am very sorry. I have to go.'

'What does it mean?' Jozef said eagerly to the professor the following day.

It was late morning. He had not had time to properly process the information he had unearthed in the records office the previous evening.

'First of all, well done,' said the professor, trying to defuse the situation as best he could.

Jozef was pacing impatiently up and down, up and down in the professor's office. 'I feel rather embarrassed that was not my first thought,' he continued, politely reprimanding himself out loud.

'I am not adopted then. My parents are wrong. They *are* my real parents,' said Jozef, still pacing.

'Jozef, please, sit down,' begged the professor. 'You are making me dizzy.'

He adjusted his bow tie, like a nervous tic and Jozef sat down.

'Let me think,' said the professor and Jozef turned to him, waiting. 'The Jozef Diederich you found can't be you, it can't be. Why would your parents tell you you are adopted? Why would they risk that – they love you very much – if it was not the truth?' he questioned, allowing thoughts to voice themselves in no real order.

Jozef remained silent and the professor steadied himself and began to nod gently. Jozef's eyes tightened in anticipation.

'I think it is you, but then of course it isn't you. It cannot be.'

Jozef only looked puzzled.

'Don't you see?' said the professor, holding his gaze. 'This is of course assuming you are adopted and that your parents were telling the truth. Do you agree they were?'

'I agree they were.'

'Good. So do I. You were adopted and I believe you are very nearly nineteen, give or take perhaps six months either way. It would be virtually impossible for you to share a birthdate with your other self. No, that cannot be,' said the professor.

Jozef was struggling to interpret his thinking.

'I do not believe your name is Jozef, nor is it Diederich. That is your adopted parents' name. Jozef must have been someone else's name. But I do believe you have a brother, not by blood. Do you understand?'

Jozef nodded, slowly at first but then more definitely with dawning clarity.

'You became Jozef Diederich the day they took you in and you stopped being who you were previously. Your adopted parents had a child and called him Jozef. He was born on March 3, 1941. You have become him, Jozef,' said the professor.

'Yes,' said Jozef, still digesting this life-changing information. 'What happened to him? And who are my real parents?'

'They are two very good questions,' said the professor. 'We must now set our minds to answering them.'

That afternoon, an immaculately attired man walked confidently into the central records office in Berlin. He expertly caught the eye of the flattered girl working the front desk.

'Good afternoon, young lady.'

'Good afternoon,' said the woman, smiling back at him.

'My name is Professor Waechter. I am from the university and doing a bit of detective work on my students – discovering what they are getting up to,' said the professor with a wink.

The lady laughed.

'My undergraduates are researching lost family members from before or during the war. One particular student of mine, who I have high hopes for, has been tasked with this assignment. Might I ask if he has been here in the last few days to research birth or adoption records in Munich from that time? His name is Diederich, Jozef Diederich.'

'I am not supposed to tell you, sir,' said the lady, who by her submissive tone was clearly about to accede to his request. 'But I can make an exception this once.'

'You are an angel,' said the man, raising his hat as the lady patted the back of her hair self-consciously.

'Yes, a Jozef Diederich has been here twice in the last few days. The second time was alone. The first was with a colleague of yours from the university I believe, a Professor Zielinski,' relayed the lady diligently.

'Professor Zielinski, you say. The swine! What were they looking for, might I ask?'

'They looked at adoption and birth records in Munich from 1935-1945.'

'Anything else?'

'No, that was it,' the woman replied.

'Thank you,' said the man. 'You have been a great help. Most kind. I hope to see you again soon.'

He doffed his hat one more time.

CHAPTER TWENTY-EIGHT

Michael's large associate did not stand easily in the cramped corridors of the history department at Berlin university.

'Do not let anyone enter,' instructed Michael.

The large man understood and clasped his hands obediently together so they hung gently in front of his frame.

Michael knocked.

'Enter,' called Professor Zielinski cheerily from behind the door to his office.

Michael entered and took off his hat as he walked confidently through.

The professor frowned. He did not recognise him.

'Yes, can I help?' the professor asked.

'Hello Professor Zielinski, my name is Michael. I have an interest in one of your undergraduates.'

The professor frowned further.

The smartly dressed man now in front of him knew his name, but had only introduced himself by his first. Michael had not asked to be seated – he had simply sat down. The professor had seen such arrogance before. He was concerned and eased his chair, conveniently on rollers, back a little towards his desk. 'Which undergraduate in particular?' enquired the professor, pretending not to be alarmed.

'Diederich, Jozef Diederich,' said Michael, resting his hands, hidden by expensive leather gloves, on his lap.

The professor noticed the gloves, and knew it was mild outside. Jozef.

His mind shifted into gear. Curiosity excited his mood and energy levels and he suddenly felt better.

'Yes, young Jozef. A charming and very capable student,' said the professor. 'We, I, have high hopes for him here at the university. It is still early days, of course, but we see wonderful potential.'

'Perhaps Herr Diederich's horizons are wider than these four walls in Berlin, professor,' said Michael.

The professor could not quickly translate Michael's last remark in his head. He let it pass and saved it for more detailed dissection later.

'Do you know Jozef?' said the professor.

It was a simple but clever question.

'Yes, I know Jozef,' said Michael, who was straining to contain his vitriol for this man, this species sat across from him.

One of the worst days of Michael's life was the day he knew the war was lost and the Third Reich lay ruined.

'What is your particular interest in Herr Diederich?' said Michael.

'My interest in Jozef is the same interest I have in all my undergraduates, Michael,' said the professor, including his name deliberately. 'He is here to study and I see potential, great potential in him.'

'Why are you helping him so much?'

The professor shifted uneasily in his seat. How did he know that? He must have good reason and the professor knew that good reason potentially led somewhere unpleasant. The detective in him was aroused again.

'Jozef needed my help. I offered it. He accepted. Quite simple. Quite innocent.'

The professor was pleased with his answer, which gave Michael frustratingly little.

Michael stood up and turned his back on the professor, placing his hat carefully on his head. The professor saw the sun highlight Michael's pale skin on the back of his neck. His hair was trimmed short. The professor realised. His heart instantly began to boom like artillery fire on the Western Front. He could only move in slow motion, like in his nightmares. He always died in the end.

The sun darted behind a cloud and the sudden change in light in the room flicked the professor back to life. Michael reacted. He swung back around, towering over the professor's frame, sunk and vulnerable below. He flicked out a long blade hidden within his right sleeve. It glinted in the glaring light, which crashed back out from behind a cloud. He pounced on the professor and swarmed on his lap like a cat with the blade decisively at his throat. Michael could have killed him right there. He wanted to and felt himself retching.

'Fucking Jude,' said Michael. 'Stanislaw Zielinski. How did you survive?'

The professor smiled. 'I did,' he said. 'I did.'

Michael kept the blade firmly, painfully at the professor's throat so the point dug into the old man's skin, breaking it and drawing delicate beads of blood. Michael knew precisely how much pressure to exert, but it had been a while. He reached down with his free hand and rolled up the professor's right sleeve. The professor let him. His hand was trapped beneath Michael. There was nothing he could do. Michael nodded. The tattoo from Auschwitz. Inimitable. It was the professor's mark. He could never take it off.

'You Jews,' crooned Michael. 'You Jews. One more less today. One more less. I would tell you to leave Jozef alone; I would tell you it doesn't matter; he won't be in Berlin, this pathetic, liberal heart of a nation next year. It doesn't matter. It doesn't matter. I am going to gut you like a dog.'

'You could,' said Stanislaw. 'You could. You Nazis could do a lot of things.'

Michael did not like the tone in his victim's voice. Experience told him it was too brave.

'My pistol in your belly will rip you in two,' revealed the professor, jabbing it hard so Michael could feel it prodding his confidence.

'We can go together,' he said. 'I will bleed out quickly. You, my friend, will die slowly. It will take ten, twenty minutes. You won't make it. I will get two, maybe three shots off. Is ten minutes enough for you to make peace with your God? I made mine a long time ago.'

Michael sneered. He wanted to vomit. He wanted to snarl. He wanted so many things. 'Jude,' he repeated. 'Fucking Jude.'

Michael pulled himself off the professor so gently it hardly felt like he was doing it.

The professor felt the release in their frames, which had been forced together tightly. He could smell Michael's cleanliness. It stank. Like God would not notice at heaven's gates, he joked in his head.

And Michael was gone.

The professor turned his eyes and head to the heavens thankfully. He let out a breath bigger than the room. His shirt was uncomfortably moist, but his old friend, his pistol, had saved him. He put it back in the bottom drawer of his desk, safely out of sight. It was a good job he had lost the key to that drawer. He smiled, shaking his head.

'Nazis. Everything's always loaded with them.'

Professor Zielinski spared Jozef from the potentially deadly nature of his meeting with Michael. 'A man came to see me yesterday,' he said. 'His name was Michael. He was very smart and polite and well-mannered,' he added.

It seemed a long time ago now. The professor had had to cancel the rest of his afternoon yesterday, but now he felt better for having done so. Today was a new day. It is amazing how resilient the human spirit is, he thought.

'Yes, I know him,' said Jozef.

The two of them were sitting on the steps to the central records office. It had been the professor's choice, and felt as good as any place to be. He had not wanted to spend time in his office today. He wanted to feel fresh air and the buzz of people flowing like water around them. Now he enjoyed the sun shining on his skin. He smiled deeply and closed his eyes and let it warm his face.

'How do you know him?' he then asked.

'I have known him longer than I can remember,' said Jozef, eating an ice cream the professor had bought him.

'He used to visit us every Thursday evening when I was child. He never missed. He came then because my mother was always out on Thursdays.'

'Professor?' asked Jozef.

'Yes?' said the professor, opening his eyes to the light.

'Why did Michael come to see you? It seems strange. He hasn't been to see me in Berlin nor has he asked my parents about me.'

'Maybe Michael takes a greater interest in you than you realise,' said the professor.

'What does that mean?'

Jozef seemed further away than ever from the truth of who he really was.

'It means you are important,' encouraged the professor and sensing Jozef was losing faith in the journey they had embarked upon together. 'You are extremely important to Michael,' said the professor. 'We know that now. We know he is prepared to do many things in your name. Travel to Berlin, for one, simply to find out how you are faring.'

'I suppose,' said Jozef downcast.

An attractive young lady glided by them. She had a skirt and high heels. Her legs looked fantastic in the light. Jozef could not help looking; the professor could not help noticing. The two of them shared a sheepish grin.

'Young men rise in the spring,' said the professor. 'Do not be ashamed Jozef. You are a young man.'

CHAPTER TWENTY-NINE

Catharina had to get out. She had to get out. Her mind was running away from her. She could not keep up. No time. No time. Gerhard would be home any minute.

She was packing a suitcase of essentials – she was leaving him. She was going to live with Janus. She did not care what people might think, the subsequent scandal. She had to get out. Gerhard would be home any minute and she could not leave if he realised – not then, not ever. It had to be today. Janus was waiting. I love him, she thought.

Catharina had written Gerhard a short letter explaining her reasons. It was pitifully little to show for more than twenty years of marriage, but it was all she had left to give. It was easier to be cruel when Gerhard was not there. Where is that blasted letter? she thought. She wanted to scream. Her bag was virtually packed. In the final rush she wanted to check that there was nothing vital she had forgotten. She could not come back here. She already had some of her nicest clothes on, she thought, catching herself in the mirror. That was a start.

The mirror pulled her back momentarily and she looked at herself. She looked old. What was she doing? Really? Leaving her husband for a younger man, a man she hardly knew if she was being truthful. Yet, she felt so close to Janus. She could say anything to him; she wanted to say everything to him. Time would help them catch up on the news of each other's lives. Gerhard would be home soon.

She dashed back to the immaculately made bed and her shabby suitcase, still lying open on top of it. She could not fit much more in. Her comb, her hairbrush. Yes, she would need those, spying them on her bedroom dresser. Catharina threw them on top and ran her hands down her skirt one last time. There was nothing else. The letter! Catharina remembered it was tucked carefully behind her dresser mirror. Gerhard would never chance upon it there, she had thought when the world seemed infinitely calmer and clearer.

It had started to rain outside. The change of weather and thick, grey sky dulled her excitement. It would have been easier to leave if the sun was shining. How ridiculous is that? she thought. Was that all this was? A summer romance, a fling that would seem childish come autumn? He would never let her live it down if she crawled back, tail curled uncomfortably between ashamed legs. The score would be even then. No, it would never be even, she determined. It could not be. How could it, after what he did, what he took from her?

Catharina had new resolve.

The rain beat down harder on the glass. It was time. Gerhard would be home any minute. She froze. She heard a car, his car, pull slowly into their driveway. He was home. She was too late. It was too late. She had failed. She could not even leave her husband properly. The sound of a car door clunking closed and heels clicking up the drive to their front door. He was here. Catharina matched them racing down the stairs - she had been quick in her youth – but strangely, the only thing she could think of now was how her best clothes would be ruined, being thrown around so violently in her suitcase. She dashed into their small kitchen and slammed the door behind her. The glass was frosted so only blurs of figures were visible. Catharina breathed again. She had her suitcase. She had herself.

'I'm home,' Gerhard announced loudly.

She felt a breeze blow through to where she stood. She was not moving.

'Darling?' Gerhard said.

He took off his coat, placed his briefcase inside the door to the living room and began to walk through to the kitchen.

'Darling?' he asked out loud again.

He began to worry. He had heard the kitchen door slam. He could see Catharina through the glass. Gerhard opened the door. Nothing. No one.

'Darling?' he said softly.

The dining table was empty bar a small envelope sat alone in its centre. Strange. The small table looked vast with only the white note anchoring its heart. One word was written on the outside. Gerhard's eyes would not let him decipher what it was until he was close.

'*Gerhard.*' Catharina's handwriting.

She stood at the end of their driveway, suitcase in hand. She had left at the last second by the back door and was crying. A neighbour walked by with his dog and saw her. Catharina started her walk to Janus' flat.

Gerhard slumped down at their table and began opening the letter painstakingly like a bomb disposal expert. He had no idea what lay inside. After he had read it, he reached inside their dining room cabinet for his best bottle of whisky, still unopened. He opened it and, in the following hours and nights, began to pour. And pour. And pour.

She had left him. How could he have been so careless with his happiness, his wife? Catharina. He saw now he hardly deserved her.

Gerhard had drunk three evenings on the spin since Catharina had left him for Janus.

At his flat she luxuriated naked beneath his wool rug, close to him and his warm frame. She could not remember the last time she had been so happy.

Gerhard meanwhile hardly ate. His appetite had deserted him like she had. He could no longer stomach food. He could not swallow. He felt he would choke if he tried.

Michael came to see him and noticed Gerhard was barely touching his whisky, which was most unlike him.

'Gerhard, it is terrible to see you like this,' he said. 'And over a whore. She does not deserve your pain, your pity. It does not become you.'

Gerhard hated the words and the cruel, empty tone, but he desperately needed someone on his side. Who else was there?

'Have you told Jozef?' asked Michael, helping himself to more whisky, which he was enjoying, although he knew he would have to go soon. He could not keep misery company for long. It was too close.

Gerhard started shaking his head disturbingly. 'No,' he said. 'I have not told Jozef. What would I say?'

'You could start by telling him that his mother is a whore and that she has left you for a Jewish dog.'

'Jozef and Catharina are so close. He would side with her,' replied Gerhard.

'You have to focus,' said Michael. 'Your job is safe, I think. The house is yours. You will not lose it if she divorces you. We still have influence in the courts. They would look kindly on your case.'

Gerhard's gaze faded in and out of the conversation. His eyes were red from a three-day hangover. He looked across and caught Michael's eyes, but he wanted to hide. He felt a failure. Abandoned. Impotent. The Diederich's front room had become claustrophobic since Catharina had left. The walls crowded in and Gerhard felt afraid. It was like Catharina had died and all she had bequeathed him was silence. Memories, possessions maybe. But nothing real. Of course, she had not died at all, but Gerhard could have accepted that. The truth that she was reborn in the world – without him, her husband – ached the most.

'I can get Catharina back,' said Michael. He had Gerhard's attention now.

'How?' he said. 'She won't listen.'

'She will have no choice.'

'What are you going to do?'

'I can eradicate the reason she left,' said Michael. 'Take that away and it is only logical that she will return. We learnt during the war that you don't have to persuade people, not really. You just give them no choice. All you have to do is say yes.'

'Yes,' said Gerhard.

CHAPTER THIRTY

Jozef and Professor Zielinski were back at the central records office in Berlin. It was quite different in daytime. Jozef had not told the professor about his scare the other night.

'Well done,' said the professor again, wrapping his arm around Jozef.

They were looking contentedly at the records of births in Munich on March 3, 1941. There he was - in plain daylight: 'Diederich, Jozef, son of Gerhard and Catharina Diederich. Born 5.30pm.'

'You really have a very clear mind,' said the professor. 'You see through problems. You certainly think differently to me. I still feel foolish I did not think of this first.'

'It's okay, professor,' said Jozef, shrugging off the praise. 'But what does it mean? I'm not really adopted after all? My parents *are* my real parents? But then why would they tell me I am adopted, especially the night before coming here to Berlin?'

'Exactly,' said the professor, removing his reading glasses. 'Why would they do that? We will assume that they believed that what they were telling you was true.'

A young woman perched herself on the edge of the table the professor and Jozef had previously exclusively enjoyed. Jozef felt it was rude to have done so without asking – his look told the professor as much. Professor Zielinski waved away the protest with his eyes and scrutinised the entry in the record books more closely.

'Do you see that? That asterisk next to your name.'

'Yes, I see it,' said Jozef. 'I did not notice it before.'

'No reason why you should. Look, there are 30 names on this page and only you, so to speak, and another boy have an asterisk next to their name. Madam?' said the professor, commandeering a lady busying herself with books. 'May I borrow you for one moment?'

She agreed and came over.

'My friend and I here are studying records of births in Munich in 1941 and were wondering what these asterisks next to particular children's names mean. There are only a few.'

The lady from the records office nodded. 'From August 1939,' she said. 'The German government decreed that all births of handicapped children had to be reported centrally.'

'Of course,' said the professor, nibbling at his reading glasses. 'Thank you, madam. You have been most helpful.'

The lady nodded and was gone.

'Let us go for a coffee and a slice of cake,' said the professor. 'Across the street at the café we enjoy so.'

Professor Zielinski relaxed into his seat outside the café and savoured his first taste of the caffeine. 'I was working on one theory concerning the real Jozef Diederich, shall we say. Now is the time to share it with you.'

'Is everything okay with your coffee and cake?' a waitress hurrying past interrupted.

Jozef thanked her and the professor smiled. He was glad to be here and glad he had begun this adventure. 'Hitler and the Nazis did not just murder Jews,' said the professor, putting his cup down for a second. 'Hitler wanted to eradicate the mentally and physically handicapped from Germany's gene pool. How did he achieve that? He murdered them. First, let me say, I don't believe that. I believe Hitler hated waste and weakness, and he saw mentally and physically handicapped Germans as weak and wasteful, a burden on society. That, I believe, is why Hitler targeted them.

'We have just learnt that from August 1939, with war only days away, all doctors had to report the birth of handicapped children,' said the professor. 'From that autumn, parents of handicapped children in Germany were encouraged to give them up and let the state care for them. It was a terrible lie. They were not cared for at all. They were killed. The deception did not end there. The families of the handicapped children were sent fictitious death certificates and an urn of human ashes.'

'I never knew,' Jozef interrupted.

'It is not something this great nation of ours is particularly proud of,' said the professor, finally starting on his cake.

Jozef had been wondering how long he could go without eating it. He then remembered he had once thought old people were a different breed, from another world. He smiled.

'What's amusing you?'

'Nothing, sorry professor.'

'I think this could explain what may have happened to the stepbrother you never met, the person you became, the person you replaced.'

Jozef then felt cold. Nobody had ever described his life in so few words before. It was the best answer yet to who he really was. A replacement. He had never truly considered the intricacies of the word before. Now that he did, he did not like it. It was a cruel, unfeeling, clinical word.

'How did people know about the children? How do you know?'

A waitress enquired if they would like more coffee.

The professor shook his head.

'Mistakes were made. The Nazis had thousands of opportunities to make errors – and they made them. Death certificates were at odds with children's medical history. Urns of ashes of boys turned up containing a girl's hair grip. The whole programme became a horrible open secret.'

'Nobody ever came back,' he continued. 'People knew. They're not stupid really. Yes, Germans were stupid enough to allow Hitler to take power, but they were not blind to what was really happening. They simply looked the other way. That is perhaps the German nation's greatest responsibility, and it must now bear it. Do you think all the hundreds and thousands of Berliners here in this grand square today, enjoying this beautiful sun, were ardent, fervent Nazis, every last one of them?'

Jozef shrugged.

'Of course not. But by their very silence they were complicit in Hitler's crimes against humanity. That is what I find hardest to forgive. I used to detest people for that.'

'What now?'

'I can help you of course, but there is something you must do alone. You must confront your adopted parents or you must confront your father's friend, Michael. Only they know the answers we seek.'

It was late, nearly midnight, at Berlin university. Professor Zielinski was in his office and wired on caffeine. He was about to make the last telephone call on a long list. He was contacting every survivor he knew and telling them to call every survivor they knew. The professor hoped the web of knowledge would spread until an answer, an identity, was unearthed. Then he would know.

'Hello,' said the voice on the end of the line blearily. It had just climbed out of bed.

'Hey, it's Stan, Stan Zielinski.'

'Stan! Hey Stan, how are you? You do realise what time it is? Are you drunk?'

'No, I'm not drunk. I'm fine,' said the professor, trying to temper his intoxication. 'I need a favour. I'm looking for someone, a former Nazi.'

The voice on the end of the line sighed. 'Stan, it's late. I don't want to talk about this now; I'm not sure I ever want to talk about it. We're not all like you. We never were.'

'I know, I know,' said the professor unperturbed. He would not be dissuaded. 'His name is Michael.'.

'His name is Michael,' said his friend. 'That's it. His name is Michael.'

'No, no,' said the professor, taking another deep gulp of coffee. 'This is a man who would have worked in the camps. He is not a military man. He is well spoken, educated, anti-Semitic like only those who worked in the camps were. He has grey hair. Blonde when he was younger. He is not a big man, slim, and he likes wearing hats and smart suits.'

'Stan,' said the voice. 'All Nazis liked wearing hats and smart suits.'

'This one is different. Someone will remember him. They must.'

'Why is it so important?'

'This man is still here, right here in Germany. He must live in or very near Munich. I'm helping someone. They need my help. They may be in danger.'

'From this man?'

'Yes, from this man,' said the professor, finishing his coffee.

'Have you asked Wojciech? He's worse than you. Hates those bastards. We all do. But not like Wojciech.'

'He was the first person I called.'

'Okay, okay. I'll ask around. Give me a few days. Don't be surprised if nothing turns up. This man is Michael. Come on, Stan.'

'Thank you. Sleep well.'

'You too,' said the voice. 'You too.'

In Munich, Michael was surrounded by three associates acquired during the war. Everyone else had failed him, either disappointingly through death or pathetically in weakness. The three men before him, all loyal beyond question, had overcome the hurdles Michael had carefully placed before them. There was nothing else after 1945, only this.

'What do we know about him?' Michael said rhetorically to the room.

The men were well versed to the opening question and knew not to answer.

'We know his name is Janus and we know he is a Pole. Poles are dangerous. We have to be careful. This is not like that man before. This is a man who might have fought. If he did, he survived and that makes him dangerous, resourceful. Those are qualities we take heart from ourselves, but qualities we respect in others.'

The three men nodded. All were still to speak. It was the way it was, the way Michael liked it. They were more intelligent than he gave them credit for. But they let him think little of them in that respect. What they did not appreciate was that Michael secretly worshipped them. They were lions in his dreams.

'She cannot be harmed,' said Michael. 'At all costs, which makes this difficult. We have to subdue them both quickly, the Pole particularly, but she could also be dangerous. I doubt it though. She will recognise me. It is time she did. We will have to keep her quiet.'

The men nodded again.

'I'll meet you here tomorrow evening, 22.00,' said Michael. 'Yes?'

'Yes, sir,' the three men said finally.

CHAPTER THIRTY-ONE

'Dad, it's Jozef,' he said in a cramped telephone box close to the university.

'Hello Jozef,' said his father, happy to hear his voice. 'I'll just go get your...' Gerhard hesitated. 'Your mother's gone out,' he added quickly. 'She is very busy with her choir these days.' He tried a cheap laugh, but could not manage it.

Jozef thought they might have had a row. He could sense unease.

'How are you?' asked Gerhard.

'Good,' said Jozef, huddled in the telephone box, which always made him feel slightly trapped.

'And university. How is university?'

'Fine. Busy, but fine. Looking forward to next year really, and getting stuck into my course more.'

'Good for you.'

Strange. Jozef had never heard his father say 'good for you' before and he thought he knew every nuance of his father's vernacular. It was peculiar to hear him suddenly talk differently. Maybe they were all growing up.

'Dad, I wanted to speak to mum. Is she around tomorrow night?'

Gerhard hesitated. 'No, more choir practice I am afraid. She really is very busy these days.'

'Okay,' said Jozef unsure himself now. He did not know what to suggest for a moment. 'The night after?'

'Yes,' said Gerhard quickly, happier now. 'I'm sure she'll be around then. I'll bloody make sure she is,' he joked. Another weak laugh.

Jozef did not reciprocate. 'Okay. I'll call back then. Auf Wiedersehen.'

Ten minutes later Gerhard had finished a modest, for him, glass of whisky. He nodded gently to himself. He had good reason to go and see her now.

He banged loudly on the dark, dead front door of the butcher's. He was sober enough, he thought.

No answer.

'Catharina!' he shouted.

A light clicked on and a face appeared. A man's. Him. Then her. Catharina. She came down and she spoke calmly to Gerhard. She was braced for drunken pleas for her to go back to him – for her to go home. She was prepared for that drama, but she was rather thrown when all he wanted was for her to be home tomorrow night to speak to Jozef. Jozef would telephone. He wanted to talk. It must be important, he said.

'Oh,' said Catharina flatly. The new thrill-seeker in her was almost disappointed. 'Have you been drinking?'

'Yes,' Gerhard conceded a little guiltily.

At least he was being honest, Catharina thought. He had not always been. Catharina then quietly laughed inside and allowed a small smile to break on her lips. What right did she now have to reprimand him about his drinking? None, she thought. You left for someone else.

It was cold. Her breath became visible, foggy white, when it left the warmth of her mouth. She wrapped her shawl around herself more tightly. It did not do much good. She was topless underneath. Gerhard would have gone mad. She tried to hold herself. Gerhard did not feel the chill. He was transfixed. He yearned desperately, hopelessly to rush forward that final step and embrace her, hold her, his wife, Catharina. But something stopped him.

A couple walked happily by across the street, laughing. It distracted them both briefly. Catharina was glad to look, but people in love pained Gerhard now. He could not handle it. It reminded him of what he had lost and thrown away, discarded. Another job done, ticked off from his list. For what, he thought suddenly. What did it matter now? What did anything matter? He had casually contemplated suicide.

'Gerhard,' said Catharina.

Nothing.

He was staring at the couple up the road.

She knew he could not see them clearly. His eyes were nowhere near good enough.

'Gerhard,' she said again. 'Gerhard!'

He stopped staring – like she had slapped him.

She made eyes at him and he did not fight them. 'Did Jozef say what time he would ring?' she asked.

'No. No, he didn't,' said Gerhard, who suddenly noticed the shawl Catharina was wearing was new. She must have bought it to impress him, he thought. 'Sorry. I did not think to ask. I was surprised he called to be honest. He doesn't often these days.'

'I'll be there,' said Catharina, feeling pity for her husband now. 'If I'm not there and he rings, tell him to call back. I want to talk to him too.'

The next evening, Catharina felt strange being back in the home she and Gerhard had made in a former life. Everything felt old and tired and infinitely less exciting than the flat she was fast transforming into a new home with Janus. There, everything made her heart jump when she saw them again first thing in the morning. Here, the drab, brown surroundings were rapidly draining her new-found happiness and patience.

'How have you been?' asked Gerhard, in the early stages of drinking for the evening.

Catharina thought it a strange question and did not know how to answer. She instead found herself inspecting their house like she was a prospective buyer, who had never seen it before. 'Fine, Gerhard,' she eventually answered.

Gerhard's heart broke a little more when she called him by his name. She hardly ever called him Gerhard – only in company or when she was very angry. Now, it was worse. She took his name coldly, like any other word. In comparison, the name Catharina meant so much to Gerhard he could not utter it now if he wanted to avoid hurting himself all over again.

Catharina wished Jozef would call. She sat down and took off her coat, wrapping it around the back of a dining room chair. It had once been a happy, busy, chaotic space. Now, it seemed small and sadly insignificant, like someone had died there once but no one cared anymore. Flowers placed to mark the spot had become carcasses.

Catharina looked stunning, thought Gerhard, draining more whisky from his glass. She had a colour to her complexion and a confidence he could not recall. He knew where she had got it from. He winced. He was straining not to grab her and hold her, kiss her, touch her, feel her. He wanted to. He *wanted* to.

The telephone rang and interrupted his desire.

Gerhard jumped, but Catharina did not move, waiting for her husband to answer. This was his home now, not hers. Gerhard got the hint and rose from his seat, but kept his whisky close.

'Hi dad, it's Jozef.'

'Hello Jozef,' said Gerhard warmly, trying to pretend his connection with their son had deepened since Catharina had left.

'Is mum there?' asked Jozef, cutting straight to business.

'Yes, she is. She is right here.'

Catharina could see what he was doing and tried not to rile. 'Hello Jozef,' she said, excited to speak to her son.

'Hi mum,' said Jozef from his bleak, untidy telephone box in Berlin.

'How are you?' she asked.

'I'm fine. Mum, I wanted to ask you something. Is that okay?'

'Of course it is, darling,' she said, lowering the telephone handle and covering it with her hand. 'Gerhard, can we have some privacy, please?'

Gerhard was uncomfortably close. He did not like to concede territory, but did not feel like pursuing the point and got up and walked out of the room. He thought he had hidden his quiet fury.

Catharina struggled to not let her temper rise, waiting impatiently for Gerhard's exit before rolling her eyes to the dining room ceiling, which had become her friend over the years. 'Sorry. What do you want to ask me?'

'I'm thinking of tracing my real parents,' said Jozef, without realising his mistake. Birth parents would have been infinitely kinder.

Catharina felt like she had been punched in the stomach and she clasped it quickly to try and nurse the discomfort. 'Yes, yes, of course,' she managed. 'What do you want to know?'

What do I want to know? thought Jozef maddeningly. I want to know who I am; I want to know everything. 'I want to know what you know about them, mum,' he said.

Mum was a good choice of words and soothed the queasiness in her belly. She knew so little, she thought, suddenly embarrassed at the lack of knowledge, the lack of anything she had had before taking on this life, this whole person.

'I, we,' she began, bringing Gerhard into the conversation. This was not her fault. 'We really know very little.'

'What is my real name?' said Jozef, horrified to ask so brutally, but feeling like his only option was to plunge straight into the dark waters waiting below.

'Jozef,' said Catharina, startled. How much did he know? 'Your name is Jozef Diederich. You were born on March 3, 1941. And that is all we know really,' said Catharina, desperately defending the lie.

'Mum, I went to the central records office in Berlin and found a Jozef Diederich born on that day to you and dad.'

Jozef was glad of the distance between himself and Catharina at this moment. If he had been in the same space as her and experienced the hurt and horror in her eyes it would have proved impossible. He would have thrown himself apologetically into her embrace and she would have immediately forgiven him. She would forgive him for everything in the end.

'Oh,' said Catharina, dulled.

Part of her great lie was exposed and defeated. She had never expected this. This moment. She had to sit down. Oh God, she thought.

Gerhard returned to the room, hoping to grab more whisky, but Catharina quickly shooed him out with a fierce face.

'Jozef,' she began, remaining seated and calm, yet sad.

Jozef sensed her anguish and ached. He wanted to hold her and tell her that he loved her, but he felt he could not in this moment. Whenever Catharina had cried when he was young, Jozef had instantly copied her and cried too. It had been an instinctive reaction. He had stopped doing it, but the pain only felt greater now that he was older. He wondered where the tears were and was afraid why they were not there anymore.

'Jozef, myself and your father had a son. He was stillborn. The complications meant I could never try for a child again.'

Catharina beat back a tidal wave of emotion. She did not know from where she summoned the strength before realising it came from the most powerful feeling she would ever experience – the unconditional love for a child. She was protecting him.

'Your real name is Jozef Drescher. You were born here in Munich on April 3, 1941 we believe, one month later. I was not happy for a long time after your stepbrother died. It helped me to think of you as my Jozef, so we gave you the same birthday. You already had the same name. We never thought of it again. Your father and I decided. It was like a miracle. You were such a happy child, even then at the end of the war.'

Jozef could see himself now – Jozef Drescher, born April 3, 1941 – for the first time. Who he was. He could almost remember. He cried finally.

'Oh Jozef,' said Catharina, who gave in herself and started to cry too.

She tried to caress and comfort her son with warm words over the line, like stroking the back of his little neck, sunburnt from happy summers in their garden.

CHAPTER THIRTY-TWO

Professor Zielinski sat in his office. It was late. He was enjoying some vodka in a coffee mug. It was deliciously decadent and helped soothe him through some tedious marking of uninspired essays.

The bottom drawer of the professor's desk was slightly ajar – not at first glance, but the professor knew. After his encounter with Michael it had become something of a safety blanket for him.

A knock at the door and the professor's pulse quickened. Who was it? It was nearly 11pm.

The professor grabbed his pistol out of his bottom drawer and tiptoed the short distance from his desk to the door, hiding behind it in case it sprang open and caught him out. His pistol was pointed, ready.

'Who is it?' the professor enquired as calmly as he could.

'Stan, it's Henryk,' said a familiar voice.

'Jesus Christ, Henryk,' said the professor, opening the door and allowing his thumping heart to beat back down. 'What are you doing here at this time?'

'Is it ever too late to see an old friend?' said Henryk warmly. 'What's with the gun?'

'It's nothing. Nothing!' protested the professor. 'Just an old man starting to lose his mind.'

Henryk could see his friend was frightened – and not much frightened him. Stan was different from most former camp inmates. He never allowed the Nazis to really reach him, not completely like the others. He retained a certain dignity. Hardly anyone did. Others foolishly tried and quickly paid with their lives, but Stan had not. He had survived and even though Henryk could have throttled him at times, he could only admire him.

'Stan, I have something for you.'

'Sit, sit,' said Professor Zielinski. 'Vodka?'

'Is the pope Catholic?' said Henryk, slapping his old friend happily.

The professor reached for another mug and poured a generous serving into it.

Henryk sat down and pulled out a book he had carefully been concealing inside his jacket. He opened it at a page he had marked. 'Is this the man, this Michael who visited you?' asked Henryk.

There he was – younger, prouder and grandly wearing a Nazi uniform. It was him, Michael. There was no mistaking those eyes. The hair was whiter and thinner now, but still in the same style, combed over to one side.

'Michael Drescher,' the professor read out. 'Chief medical officer of Hadamar State Institution and Sanatorium. Well, well. As I live and breathe. Well done!' exclaimed the professor, wrapping an arm around his friend's shoulder, who was enjoying the vodka which had begun to draw a giddy smile across his lips. 'What is this? How did you get it?'

'It is what the Nazis called a death book. It holds all the records from Hadamar, one of six centres set up to house and kill the mentally and physically handicapped from 1940-42,' he said. Henryk flicked through the pages and underlined a figure with the tip of his finger. 'Here,' he said.

Professor Zielinski leaned in for a closer look. There it was, plain and clinical. The Nazis got their numbers right at least. The professor shook his head and drank some vodka. It was hard to think of such numbers and translate them into people the Nazis had targeted and then eliminated with murderous efficiency.

Henryk read, 'Hadamar: in operation from January 1941 to July 31, 1942. People processed: 10,072. Total: 10,072.'

'Ten thousand,' said the professor. 'Ten thousand. Poor bastards. Thank you so much for this. Can I keep it for a few days? I will bring it back to you in person. You have my word. I will guard it with my life.'

'I know you will,' said Henryk. 'Where can an old man get a good drink and a warm bed around here?'

'I know just the place,' said the professor, rising to his weary feet, knees cracking.

The men wrapped their arms around one another and walked out of the office.

'It is what the Nazis called a death book, Jozef,' said the professor the next day. 'It is priceless. It must remain in safe hands. It was in the possession of a fellow survivor and now it is temporarily in my possession.'

'Where is it from?' asked Jozef.

The two of them were sitting in the professor's office. It was a brilliant morning, not yet 9am and the formal start of the university day.

The professor had not been able to wait; he was too intoxicated by the knowledge. 'It is from a place called Hadamar,' said the professor. 'One of six killing centres created by the Nazis in early 1940 and in open operation until the summer of 1942. Together, more than 70,000 mentally and physically handicapped Germans, Aryan Germans – these were not Poles or Slavs or Russians or Jews – were secretly murdered under direct orders from Hitler.'

'Why?' said Jozef.

'Darwin,' said the professor. 'The survival of the fittest. The Nazis called it "life unworthy of life". Hitler knew he could not carry out such work publicly. He knew he would have opposition at home from the Catholic Church and he knew the Allies would use the knowledge and very probably win the propaganda war with it. But the Nazis were not alone in adopting these ideas. In the USA from the start of the century up to 1939, more than 30,000 men and women deemed unfit to have children were sterilised by the government. Many were forced. Others did not know. Of course, Hitler took Darwin's ideas a significant step further and he did not allow nature to take its course. He began a genocide against handicapped people in Germany.

'From early 1934, only a year after Hitler became chancellor, Germany began sterilising between 300,000 and 400,000 physically and mentally handicapped German men and women. A Marriage Law was passed a year later in 1935 so couples had to prove that they would not pass hereditary diseases on to their children.'

A knock at the door. The secretary of the modern history department peeped her head around it. 'Professor, there is an undergraduate to see you. A Frau Kluge,' she said.

The girl who spoke too much.

'Tell her I'm busy all morning. I can see her if she can come back early this afternoon,' he answered curtly.

The secretary nodded and expertly closed the door behind her without making a sound.

'Jozef,' said the professor, holding Jozef's eyes with his own, 'the man you know as Michael, the man you knew growing up, ran Hadamar for the first year of its existence, until spring 1941.'

The professor revealed Michael's photograph on a separate sheet of paper tucked towards the back of the book. It was not officially part of it.

Jozef stared at it, Michael's head and shoulders proudly looking back from the small, passport-style window in the top corner of the page. Jozef nodded slowly. He did not feel anything. He was too busy thinking, piecing together clues in his head.

Michael was a malevolent, intelligent man, who had dominated his father during his childhood. He now knew why. Gerhard was not capable of this, overseeing the murder of more than 10,000 people. It rang true that Michael would be so precise, so correct, so particular.

Jozef picked up a glass of water from the professor's desk and drank from it for a moment.

The professor allowed Jozef to ingest the information. He thought he might have been upset. He was surprised he was not. Still, it was a lot to process. The professor did not say anything, but instead watched his understudy closely, discreetly. He wanted him to be okay. He wanted it to be okay.

Jozef then noticed Michael's name. He had been too busy focused on those eyes, trying to magically elicit some clandestine truth from the tiny portal to the past. He felt Michael was trying to tell him something. His name. Jozef read it again: 'Dr Michael Drescher.'

He lost control of himself. His limbs could not do anything, as if he had fast forwarded 70 years to the body of an ancient man, broken and fragile at the end of existence. Jozef's grip loosened and the glass of water fell to the floor. It hit the carpet and bounced. Jozef watched. Water spilled out onto the green material.

The professor immediately bent down to pick it up.

'Oh God,' said Jozef, though he had hardly heard the words. 'Oh God,' he said again, louder now. 'Professor, my name, my real name.'

'What Jozef?' asked the professor, concerned.

Jozef looked pale like weak light.

The professor struggled to discern the difference between the two. Only Jozef's protruding nose and eyes clearly distinguished him in all the white. The professor put his hand up to shield his eyes momentarily. 'What Jozef?' he said again. 'What?'

'My name, my real name,' he repeated. 'My mother told me last night that my real name is Jozef Drescher. I was born April 3, 1941, one month after Jozef Diederich, who was stillborn.'

The professor's eyes panicked, trying but failing to translate his friend's revelation.

Jozef's colour then returned.

'Michael Drescher. Dr Michael Drescher.'

'The coincidence is too much, isn't it?'

'I don't know,' said the professor, who instinctively thought it was. He had learnt not to believe in coincidences. 'Let us not be hasty, but, yes, it is perfectly possible that Michael Drescher is your father.'

The professor tried to place a hand on his student's sagging shoulder. It did not help.

It is too beautiful today to be unhappy, thought Jozef. He wanted to it to be grey and wet and miserable. He would have been happier then.

Another knock at the door. It was the department secretary again, opening the door widely now. She was becoming annoyed. It was 9.30am. People were beginning to queue.

'Professor?' she said abruptly.

'I know, I know,' agreed the professor, irritated. 'Let's go out Jozef.'

Jozef did not say anything. He was still too stunned.

'We are going out Frau Kirsch. I will be back this afternoon. It is very important,' he said. 'I am afraid everyone will have to wait.'

Professor Zielinski whirled on his tweed jacket and helped Jozef to his feet, handing him his briefcase as he did so.

Jozef looked like he would have clean forgotten it otherwise and Jozef never forgot anything, thought the professor.

'Come on,' he comforted him, supporting him past a stream of students in the narrow corridor leading out of the department and out of the building, out into the world.

Clean air.

Jozef did not say anything. He kept his head bowed. Fellow undergraduates thought something strange was happening. Jozef did not know who he was, who he had become and who he would become. Who was he? Michael. Those eyes, staring back at him from history and the small portrait photograph in the top corner of the document. 10,072. 10,072. Was Michael a victim too? Was it not really him? Or him in another time, another place?

Professor Zielinski and Jozef walked out together into the dazzling white. It did not hit them happily. The professor felt he was hauling a vampire out into the world to prove sunlight would not burn him alive.

'There is a café just down here,' said the professor, still propping up a shell-shocked Jozef. 'Hardly anybody uses it.'

Five minutes later the professor was pouring coffee more happily.

It was true, there was no one else here, thought Jozef, sipping water and slowly coming around.

'We will discover if Michael is your real father,' said the professor. 'First, do you want to know what kind of man he really was? What he did?'

No reply. No indication from Jozef. He was thinking, but his mind had forgotten how.

'Jozef, this is important, quite important,' said the professor and Jozef began to nod his head in response.

The professor paraphrased from the death book he still had in his possession, 'The Nazis appointed Michael to run Hadamar. Michael had prospered because many in the medical profession were opposed to Hitler's policy of killing the mentally and physically handicapped. Michael was not. He was not a real doctor, it is believed, but no matter. He could be trusted, the Nazis thought. They seemed right to have thought so.' The professor paused to sip coffee.

The sun slid briefly behind the clouds.

The change of light was a relief to Jozef.

'Michael has written here. Families of patients received three letters to convince them of the lie. The first told them that their relative had been transferred for 'war purposes'. A second told them that they had arrived at Hadamar and gave them visiting times and so forth. A third letter told them that they had died. Michael has added here as a footnote that it is wise patients are processed within 24 hours of arrival to avoid mistakes, like relatives trying to visit. That could ruin everything, he adds.

'Michael has kept copies of letters he sent to Berlin, praising members of staff at the institute and suggesting that they could be useful to the Party when a final solution to the Jewish question had been reached. He further recommends the transfer of gas chambers from Hadamar for use in larger camps in the future.'

Jozef began to feel a chill. He looked up and hoped the sun would come back out.

'Michael worked out how much money processing the first thousand patients at Hadamar had saved the Party,' said the professor. 'There is a picture,' he added, handing Jozef a photograph. In it, people were happy, smiling and had glasses full of drink in their hands. They were posing.

The professor read blankly, 'A picture of staff celebrating the 10,000th patient processed at Hadamar. Senior staff had wine. Junior team members each received a small bottle of beer, Michael writes. Staff then gathered in the basement to witness the burning of the body. They first decorated the corpse with flowers before loudly applauding when it was time for the cremation. Michael is not in the photograph. That is not the end. There is more.'

The professor ordered more coffee.

'Do you want to know Jozef, really know, what type of man Michael was? The man, do not forget, who it is perfectly possible is your biological father.'

'I want to know,' said Jozef. 'This is who I am.'

The professor shook his head. 'Jozef,' he said, taking his hand and wrapping his own around it like a blanket. 'You are not your father, whoever he is and most certainly – most certainly – not like this man.

'Is everything good with your coffee?' a waitress asked suddenly. She glanced at Jozef and saw how handsome he was.

'Everything is perfect, young lady,' he said. 'Danke.'

He began again, 'At Hadamar, Michael oversaw experiments. He starved children and he measured the results. He gave them electric shock therapy for wetting the bed. In spring 1941, just over a year later, the Nazis reassigned Michael and asked him to give lectures to troops, handpicked to be part of killing squads on the Eastern Front, the *Einsatzgruppen*. There were initially four of them. Michael was attached to the first of them, Einsatzgruppen A. Each Einsatzgruppen consisted of between 500 and 800 men.

'The normal rules of warfare did not govern them. They operated behind the frontline, away from regular German troops, and they killed Jews. Senior Nazis decided it would be bad for morale if other soldiers witnessed what they were doing. Hitler wanted Michael to observe the psychological impact on the men in Einsatzgruppen A, the psychological impact of killing Jews in large numbers every day.'

The last words made Jozef stop. It was impossible to grasp the enormity of what they had done.

'The Nazis knew from Hadamar that Michael was both meticulous and an excellent record keeper. Michael recorded precisely how many Jews Einsatzgruppen A killed behind the frontline in two years of operation, before things started to go badly on the Eastern Front for the Nazis.'

'337,' said the professor.

Jozef took the figure in. 337 did not sound so bad in the context of the Second World War where millions had perished.

'Per day,' added the professor. '337 per day. For two years.'

Jozef had a mouth full of cola and nearly choked. He began coughing violently. The professor realised he was in some discomfort and sprang up from his seat across the small, round table they occupied. Neighbouring patrons glanced across at them. Professor Zielinski slapped Jozef's back and Jozef began to regain his breath.

'Are you okay?'

'Yes, I'm okay,' he croaked, gradually regaining his voice. His throat burnt from the slug of liquid which had scythed down the moment he had heard the professor's last statement.

'Professor?' asked Jozef. 'How many did they kill in two years?'

'Einsatzgruppen A, B, C and D, who did not total 3,000 men, killed more than one million in two years of operation behind the Eastern Front. Could we have some water, please?' the professor said to the girl waiting on tables outside the café.

'There is a report Michael has written here,' continued the professor. 'It is about what he observed during those two years. He signs it 'Dr. D'. It reads, 'I found myself confronted by a tremendous grave. People were closely wedged together and lying on top of one another so their heads were visible. Nearly all had blood running over their shoulders from their heads. Some were still moving. Some were lifting their arms and turning their heads to show they were still alive. I estimated the grave contained 1,000 people. One of the men was doing the shooting. He sat at the edge of the great grave, his feet dangling. He was smoking a cigarette. People, naked, climbed into the pit and clambered over the heads of people lying there to the place the shooter directed them. Some caressed those still alive and spoke to them in a low voice. I walked away and noticed another truck load of people had arrived. I drove in my car back to camp'.

'The next morning I again visited the site. I saw 30 people lying naked near the pit, 30 to 50 metres away. Some were still alive. They had a fixed stare and seemed to not notice the chill. I moved away from the site. I heard shots from the pit. The Jews who were still alive had been ordered to throw the last corpses into the pit. Then they had themselves to lie down in it to be shot'.'

CHAPTER THIRTY-THREE

It was dark. Hushed.

Michael stood in the street, which was deserted, with his three associates. One of them was picking the lock to the door to the butcher's beneath Janus' flat. Another had patiently kept watch outside all afternoon and confirmed Janus and Catharina were now safely inside and vulnerable.

A street light overhead was uncomfortably bright, highlighting their activity to the world if it was watching.

'Come on, come on!' hissed Michael.

This was critical. It was his side of the bargain he had made with Gerhard. His reward was Jozef.

'Sir,' said one of the men. He had spotted someone, walking a dog late at night. He was approaching from 50 yards. He was not altering his course.

'Scheisse!' said Michael. 'Come on, come on!'

The door clicked open and the three men flooded inside. Michael quickly followed, immediately closing the door behind him. Michael would have happily cut the man's throat. Jozef, he thought. The men crept silently through the butcher's shop, which was dead to the world. None of them spoke. There was moonlight, macabrely shining on the hanging carcasses. The men reached the back of the premises and saw the stairway pointing up to Janus' flat. Michael nodded so gently he would have calmed a baby. Two men led the group up the narrow staircase. Michael tightened the gloves on his hands. This was it. Jozef. The door was unlocked. The three men looked back in unison at Michael. He nodded again, more aggressively. 'Now, now. Now!' he screamed.

Inside, Catharina thought some maniac was shooting at them when the door to Janus' flat banged violently open. Terror. Hot panic. Voices. Angry, urgent voices. Then foreign footsteps, heavy and aggressive.

'Janus!' she cried.

The first two strangers through the door bolted for him.

Catharina watched, groggy and disbelieving.

The nightmare was very real. The intruders' bulk flashed in and out of the moonlight peering in from the street outside.

Catharina sat up. She was in bed, naked and exposed bar her best silk undergarment, protecting her below her delicate waist. Her stomach quickly started to curdle like milk in summer heat.

Two men hauled Janus out of bed. The strongest had him in a chokehold. He struggled to breathe. That beautiful mouth.

'Get off him. Get off him! What do you want?' Catharina said, tears flooding her plea.

Before she knew it a third man enveloped her, ripping her violently from her paralysis. He hauled her roughly like coal down the side of the bed. She was a doll, helpless. She stole a look across to Janus. Her absent focus meant she failed to cushion her fall from the bed. She banged her shoulder and deep, throbbing pain dulled her senses momentarily. She could not let it distract her. It was unimportant. Janus.

He sat lifeless on the floor. The man in front had a blade to his throat. He was utterly outflanked. The third man dragged Catharina across the floor, so she was forced to break her gaze from Janus. She did not want to. If something happened to him while her eyes were selfishly elsewhere she would never forgive herself.

The stranger towered over her, suddenly lascivious. Catharina realised she was topless. Her pretty breasts had tumbled out of bed with her. He was admiring them. She frantically tried to cover them with her hands and arms. She could not be sure she was doing a good job. He continued admiring. Rape would have been easier to stomach. She could not see Janus. Where was he? Then she saw him. Michael. Smiling, staring. She was exactly where he had always wanted her.

'You bastard,' she said.

'Guten Abend Catharina,' he said.

'I won't go back,' she said instinctively. 'I won't go back. I know he sent you.'

Janus gurgled, struggling for breath on the other side of the bed, which separated the lovers like an ocean.

'Leave him alone. Leave him alone!' she protested.

Catharina tried to climb to her feet. Two huge hands forced her down easily. It was useless. Her breasts were visible again. She could see Michael enjoying them. She felt sick. He relished her reaching for something, anything to cover herself with one hand while the other tried desperately to block her chest from sight. Michael had seen enough. He took off his coat and wrapped it around her. She momentarily considered ripping his face from his skull with her teeth when he was close.

'What do you want? I won't go back. I know he sent you.'

Michael began to nod and half shake his head at the same time. He almost found her sexier now that she wore his coat. He felt erect. 'I have seen Gerhard,' said Michael. 'He is not gut. He needs you Catharina. He is a weak man. This you know.'

'I know my husband,' she said fiercely. 'Do you think I have been stupid all these years? I know exactly who you are.'

'Evidently not,' said Michael, taking a seat behind her.

The room was in good order. Control. Power. Those Jews, his imagination interrupted and Michael half smiled.

Catharina was profoundly afraid. Fear began to overtake her anger and she thought about trying to climb to her feet again, but the man in front of her motioned forward half a step.

Michael raised his hand to ward him off. 'I am not here for your husband,' said Michael. 'Do you think I care?'

Catharina had always secretly believed he had not, but she could see it clearly now. If only Gerhard was here, she thought. 'I'm going to tell the authorities,' said Catharina. 'They'll hang you for what you did.'

'Yes, they would,' said Michael, relaxing into the situation and about to remove his gloves before realising that would be an error.

'You would only be wasting their time. I am ready to leave Germany. No one would see me again. I am quite certain. This is not my Germany anymore,' he added with bile and realised he had dropped his guard. He rose to his feet, annoyed.

Catharina could see it.

'Catharina, my darling, I am not here for your pathetic husband. I am here for your son – my son. Jozef.'

He smiled again.

She realised now. She shook her head. How had she not seen? 'I don't believe you,' she said, desperately trying to tidy away the revelation like plates after dinner. 'You picked up Jozef off the street. He is probably a Jew, some orphan of all those poor people you killed, you murdered.'

'Do you think I would have one of those dogs in my house, at my table?'

'Why do you hate so much?'

Michael did not answer.

The man guarding Catharina was also intrigued. He followed orders, people like Michael's orders. He had not questioned. He questioned now whether Michael did.

'Why not?'

'But why?'

'I am here for my son,' he said, turning away and placing the chair he had found exactly where he had discovered it. 'Jozef is so much bigger than you and Gerhard, you cannot understand,' he said. 'You will never understand. There is so much emotion in this world. You seem to play with it like a kitten. It is not a toy. It has power. National Socialism learned how to harness that power, that was all.'

The stranger who had been guarding Catharina retreated from his post and flanked Michael, who nodded. The man crouched in front of Janus forcefully plunged his blade into his tight stomach and ripped a terrible tear along its front. The man behind Janus then released his vice-like hold of his neck. The four were gone. Catharina screamed. Blood. Pouring, dripping, wasting, leaving. Blood. More blood.

Catharina scrambled across to Janus and desperately tried to hold his stomach in. Her hands felt like they were trying to halt the tide. It was hopeless. She began to cry uncontrollably like a child. Janus smiled sadly. He motioned her forward and whispered in her ear. 'Don't cry. Don't cry.'

A chill cloaked Janus' naked frame, like Death was behind him, waiting patiently. 'Vodka,' Janus gurgled.

Catharina stumbled to her feet. She was dressed in blood and more red than pale, white skin. She clumsily clutched the bottle of spirits and crouched back next to Janus, sat lifeless, leaking violently onto the floor of the flat. She began to pour. She was shaking.

Janus opened his mouth. Little went in. He was moaning and slipping into eternity, black beneath him like an abyss. He wanted to fall. Adrenalin would not let him. He gurgled again, moaning.

Stop it, Catharina's head screamed and she began crying again. 'Janus,' she said. 'Stay with me! Stay with me sweetheart. You're not going to die. You're not.'

Deep moaning again. It was not him.

The grotesquely guttural sound vibrated through Catharina's fragile frame, choking her heart. It drilled into her. She could not reach back down and pull its horrors out. She cried again. She cried. Catharina poured more vodka.

Janus opened his mouth to receive it. He passed back into unconsciousness. Warmth enveloped him. Janus liked that. He died.

CHAPTER THIRTY-FOUR

Jozef was happily busying himself tidying his room. He had done well enough throughout the year in his essays to be exempt from end of year exams. He had done it. He had made it through year one. The summer beckoned and then a shared house in his second year in Berlin with Mathias, Martyn and Pierre, out of university halls and out of this place, this room. Jozef was almost going to miss its drab, scratched features. It looked different now he was emptying it of his things. It began to resemble how it had looked when he had first entered it at the start of the academic year, a lifetime ago now. But there were too many memories between the four walls for it to ever be quite the same again.

Pierre had urinated drunkenly into Jozef's sink one night when he was too intoxicated – or too lazy – to stagger the few yards to the end of the corridor and the bathroom. Jozef did not mind in the moment, although once he had got Pierre safely out of his room, he had scrubbed his little sink for Germany the next day through the hot haze of a hangover.

A knock at the door.

Strange. His parents were not due for another two days to take him home to Munich. Everyone else he knew was consumed, cramming for exams which had to be passed to safely secure passage to the next academic year.

Jozef walked over to the door, wiping hands dusty from cleaning as he did so on a cloth, which had become rather too grubby to think about. Jozef put the thought out of his mind. He opened the door. Michael.

'Jozef,' he said, doffing a dashing hat. 'How are you my boy?'

'Michael,' said Jozef somewhat downbeat. He was surprised and exposed. There was no third person to dilute any discomfort between them – and what was he doing here?

'Good to see you,' said Jozef, trying to raise his spirits.

'May I come in?'

'Of course. Come in.'

Michael entered the small room and was instantly underwhelmed. He tried badly to hide the emotion. 'So this is it,' he said. 'Where the future brains of Germany are forming new ideas and policy.'

'This is it,' said Jozef.

Michael's grandness seemed out of place here. Discomfort. The two of them shared the space uneasily. Jozef had no real idea what to say. Michael immediately sensed it. 'Have you eaten?' he said. It was 1pm.

'No, I haven't eaten,' said Jozef.

'Shall we go out for lunch? I'm famished.'

'Okay,' agreed Jozef, feeling at least that broken company with strangers in a restaurant would help bridge the barrier between them.

'Lead the way,' said Michael cheerily. 'I know just the place.'

'Shall we order?' said Michael after they had reached the café. It was a bright, bustling day in the capital. People were happy.

'What would you like sir?' asked a waitress.

'I will try your steak sandwich and some coffee, please,' said Michael, fanning himself. The heat was rising. It was hitting the middle of the afternoon.

'Jozef?' asked Michael, inviting him to order, which only riled him. He hated being mothered, while larger thoughts of what he and the professor now knew of Michael made him retch. How could he eat?

'I'll have trout and salzkartoffeln please,' said Jozef. 'And a glass of cola.'

Michael smiled, recalling the nights when Jozef sat and dozed while he and Gerhard had talked and drank and listened to the wireless. The past was never coming back, Michael thought surrounded by all this – this joy. He detested it.

His associate was poised 100 yards away, keeping a discreet eye on his paymaster.

Drinks arrived and Michael and Jozef enjoyed their first mouthfuls. Any wind had died away and people populating central Berlin's main square were trapped in the sun's full glare.

Michael placed his hat back on for protection.

Jozef shifted his position slightly so the tip of a nearby building cast the top of his face in shadow.

'How is university?' said Michael. 'Everything going well I trust.'

'Good, good, thank you Michael,' said Jozef, politely on guard. 'I have managed to be exempt from my end of year exams, so I am already through to my second year.'

'Excellent, excellent,' said Michael and Jozef instinctively felt hurt Michael had not congratulated him instead.

'Are you in Berlin for business?'

Michael paused. He had to find the right words.'Yes,' he said. 'I am here on business.'

Jozef was reaching the end of his plate of food. He had largely finished his salzkartoffeln, but he still had a piece of trout remaining. His stomach was starting to tighten. He would have a break, he thought and he placed his knife and fork neatly by the side of his plate.

A waitress nearby thought he had finished. 'Have you finished?' she enquired, hardly awaiting an answer before beginning to clear away his food.

'No, I haven't finished,' interrupted Jozef.

Michael smiled. He liked to see Jozef assert himself, a young man in Berlin. It reminded him of someone.

'Jozef,' said Michael, finishing his food and dabbing the sides of his mouth with a thick, white napkin provided by the cafe. 'There is something I want to tell you, something I have wanted to tell you for a very great time.'

Jozef tensed hopelessly. The calories were starting to swell uncomfortably in his belly, exacerbating his acute discomfort. Michael was going to tell him. This is what Jozef had wanted to know. Now he was here, Jozef did not want to hear it... Maybe Gerhard had had the right idea all along, hiding him from the truth.

'Jozef,' said Michael again.

No, protested Jozef's mind. But there was no stopping now.

'I am your real father,' he said, half reaching out a hand.

Jozef quickly retreated his.

Michael saw.

'I know this is a terrible shock,' he continued, removing his hands from the centre of the space separating them. 'I know your parents told you that you were adopted. And I congratulate you on handling such a shock so maturely in your first year away from home. I am proud of you Jozef,' said Michael, removing his hat.

He needed some air and he wanted to remove every possible barrier between them. Jozef experienced a retching sensation again. He wanted the waitress to scoop up his trout from in front of him. Jozef smelt it rotting. He had finished his cola and had nothing else to dampen his throat. He needed water. Where was the waitress?

'Thank you Michael,' said Jozef, who felt gruesomely ashamed to have won the pride of a war criminal, free from justice and free from the baying army of all the ghosts he had conspired to extinguish.

Michael hated Jozef using his name. No, he had to be patient. Give him time, he thought.

'What are you thinking?' Michael asked.

I don't know, thought Jozef. I don't know! What was he supposed to think? Jozef began to curse himself mentally for not being better prepared. He wished the professor was here. He would know what to say. 'I don't know,' said Jozef. 'I don't know Michael. It is a lot.'

That word again – 'Michael'.

Michael fought back bile rising up his spine from the darkness, circling like sharks below.

'I understand, I understand,' Michael muttered, betraying his impatience.

Jozef sensed it and only felt more uneasy. He was trapped. Suffocating. Where was that waitress? The sun was so hot and the smell of rotting fish from below was filling him with nausea. He felt the past rushing to the surface. 'Michael,' he said. 'Can I ask you some questions about the war to help me at university?'

'Of course you can,' agreed Michael, glad to establish any foothold in the uncomfortable canyon between them.

'What was a Nazi concentration camp?'

Jozef was impressed with his detachment. Keep it short, he told himself, remembering the professor's best advice.

'It is always important, in my experience, to think of these things in literal, simple terms,' Michael began. 'A concentration camp was simply that – a concentration of people in a camp, a work camp. National Socialism believed – and I did not argue with it – that certain sections of German society had lived a decadent lifestyle between the wars. After the Depression, it was time for that to stop. The National Socialists made society productive again.'

'Why couldn't those people be given normal jobs in factories or offices?'

'Special times called for special measures,' said Michael, drinking a little wine to wash down his lunch. 'Herr Hitler was not afraid of getting tough.'

'Who did he get tough with?'

'Lots of people. Political enemies like communists and Jews to begin with.'

'Jews,' repeated Jozef.

Michael finished his wine rather too quickly and hurriedly ordered a second glass. It was unlike him at lunch. He took a mouthful as soon as it arrived. The waitress began to tidy things up on their table, but Michael impatiently waved her away. His sharks were circling in.

'What did you do during the war?' asked Jozef.

Bad question.

Michael drank some more. He was starting to feel it – the intoxication was whirling in his head and clouding his senses.

'Jozef,' said Michael, trying to compose himself. 'We all did things we would rather forget during the war. Everyone who lived through it here in Berlin alive today did something they regret to survive. We survived. We are the survivors.'

'What did you do to survive?' asked Jozef.

Such determined questioning was not in his nature. But he was doing well; he could feel Professor Zielinski whispering encouraging words in his ear.

'I worked in a hospital.'

'A normal hospital?'

'It was a special hospital for the mentally and physically handicapped. Cripples, spastics. During the war we needed to care for them, keep them out of the way, to release society from the burden and allow people, normal, productive people, to focus on the war effort. Winning was all that mattered.'

'I think I have found you,' said Jozef, suddenly producing the death book from Hadamar. He placed it on the table framing the gulf between them. He pushed it forward slightly.

Michael retreated.

'You were at a place called Hadamar.'

Professor Zielinski was at Jozef's side now, cheering him on.

Michael continued to recoil.

'Here you are. That is you, isn't it? Dr Michael Drescher? Dr D on a lot of these papers.'

Michael looked back at his tiny portrait. A ghost in his National Socialist uniform. His past was sat in front of him; in front of all these people, happy, enjoying lunch and wine and beer and coffee. 'Yes,' said Michael gently. 'That is me.' It was time. It was time. 'I want you to come and live in South America with me.'

'South America?' said Jozef alarmed. 'What do you mean, South America? My whole life is in Germany. My future.'

'You will have friends in South America. New friends, important friends, people who can give you opportunities. You would be able to achieve things. Think about it.'

'Why South America?' Jozef asked again.

'It is the last place where we can rise, where we can build again,' said Michael, looking beyond Jozef. He was picturing it. The power.

'The last place? The last place to build what?'

'We are already out there, creating jobs, doing business, in government. Our friends could not have greater power. You will be able to realise your potential Jozef. You have great potential.'

'I've just finished my first year at university. Why can't I achieve my potential in Germany? I think I'd like to write Michael – newspapers.'

'There are newspapers in South America too.'

CHAPTER THIRTY-FIVE

Catharina was alone in the dining room she had shared with Gerhard for all those lifetimes. She had sat there quietly thinking, contemplating since early afternoon. She felt hollow now she was back. She hated this place. She hated him. No, more than that. She *loathed* him. She wanted him dead for what he had done. She knew she did not have murder in her, but what did she have in her? She wanted to find out.

Catharina heard the front door open and click gently shut. It was Gerhard. He was home. She could hear him, like clockwork, place his briefcase carefully down by his feet before removing his raincoat and hanging it on the same hook as always. She heard her husband then open the door to his study and place his briefcase by his desk for the night, waiting to be collected again first thing in the morning. She fleetingly felt she had never been away and almost shuddered. She was not that person anymore. She had changed. She was different. The furnishings surrounding her now looked like they belonged to another time entirely.

Gerhard appeared and was startled. He had not been expecting her. 'You made me jump,' he said, standing there, scared to intrude further into the space.

Catharina was guarding the room like a lioness ominously protecting her young. She did not say anything.

He wanted her to say something. Say something, he repeated impatiently in his head.

The tired clock on their tatty mantelpiece struck 6pm, but the cold war between them continued. I am not going to bail him out, Catharina thought. He can speak first.

She wanted to know what he was going to say, what he could say after what he had done, after all he had done. She felt her throat burn with fury. She was thirsty, but she did not want to move and abandon her position, her sanctity. Her heart was beating in her chest, a chest he would never touch, never caress again, so softly. Rising bile began to replace the burn – more corrosive. She was struggling to breathe. Her heart felt like it was about to explode. Why would he not say something? She wanted him to say something. Say something, her head screamed. Say something!

Catharina then launched herself at Gerhard like a twister, terrifying, out of nowhere. She rushed at her husband. Again and again. Pent up fury, dormant for decades, now flew out, possessing her, overwhelming her – overwhelming him.

Gerhard whimpered under the weight of the assault, cowering and holding his arms and hands up meekly to protect his head. He was pathetic, she thought. Pathetic. Pathetic. He whimpered again and began to cry.

Catharina thumped and smashed down on him like she was beating a drum.

Gerhard collapsed.

She had never hit him before. The sensation was unreal. She forgot who she was briefly. She thought of Janus, her beautiful Janus, drifting into death and all that blood. His grotesque rattles regurgitated inside her chest and she relaunched her assault on her husband with a scream.

Catharina then caught herself. It took Gerhard several seconds to realise the blows were no longer pouring down on his position from above. Smiling down on her from the mantelpiece. Her perfect little boy. He must have been two. Just before maybe. Catharina's first sobs made her whole chest heave – like someone was releasing an ancient valve letting off rusted steam. She buckled. Her lungs gasped from the effort and sheer emotion of her assault. She crumpled into a ball on the floor next to her husband. He was still whimpering and she looked at him and did not hate him so fiercely for a moment. She felt sorry for him instead.

Two dice lay curiously on the carpet, hidden underneath an armchair. They were from a favourite game Jozef and Catharina had played for hours on end when he was very little. He did not really understand the rules, but he had loved it unconditionally all the same. Catharina remembered how he had cried for hours when they had lost the dice. Gerhard had searched the house for days and weeks after their disappearance until failing memory allowed them to forget.

She picked them up now and put them away routinely, back where they belonged.

Catharina looked down again on her husband crouched in a foetal position, like he was praying, rocking gently. His whimpering had quietened. Jozef, Catharina recalled again. Tears welled out of her eyes.

'Why?' she said. 'Why, Gerhard? Why? You murdered our son. My son. Why?'

'I don't know,' he said quietly. 'I'm sorry. I'm sorry. It was a different time – remember? Anything seemed possible. Things became better, didn't they?'

'He was only a little boy,' she said, louder. 'Our little boy, Gerhard, ours! Not yours. Not the Party's. Ours. You killed him. You killed him.'

Catharina began slapping her hands down on her husband again. He yelped pathetically and quickly tried to cover himself, bringing his arms and hands up over the top of his frame. Her assault had less energy this time.

'I couldn't handle it. I couldn't handle it, alright!' Gerhard confessed. 'Couldn't you see? You couldn't handle this anymore, could you? You left. You killed our marriage. We're even.'

'You bastard. You bastard,' she said with tears inflaming her tone. 'We are never even Gerhard! Never! Do you understand? Do – you – understand?'

'Yes,' he said weakly. 'Yes.'

CHAPTER THIRTY-SIX

'Gerhard and Catharina had a little boy,' said Michael. 'He was also called Jozef. He was a month older than you.'

'I know,' said Jozef. 'He was stillborn. Mother couldn't have children after that.'

'That's not strictly true.'

An elderly lady knocked clumsily into their table, making Michael spill coffee down his blazer.

'I do beg your pardon, gentlemen,' the lady apologised. 'I am so very sorry.'

Michael fixed a fake, forced smile across his face. He would have happily slit her throat and Jozef sensed Michael's furious unease.

'What do you mean?' he said. 'What is not true?'

'Gerhard and Catharina did indeed have a son and named him Jozef before you. But he was not stillborn. He was a cripple. He had a condition called cerebral palsy.'

'But he died in birth?' said Jozef, off-balance for the first time in the exchange.

'He died early in life. He was four. There was a war to be won and Gerhard was under a very great deal of pressure. I helped take the pressure off your parents.'

'What happened to my stepbrother?' said Jozef.

Michael searched carefully for the words.

Jozef could see him thinking hard.

'He died in an institution during the war,' said Michael. 'Of pneumonia. I helped your parents place him in that very great institution. The initial transition proved too much for him. He was weak. He did not survive.'

'I don't believe you,' said Jozef.

Michael was shocked.

Jozef had never questioned his authority before.

'Jozef, I understand this is difficult. But it happened. It was a very different time. It is hard for people who did not live through that time to understand.'

Michael sipped some more coffee but flustered he spilt it down his chin. 'Scheisse!' he whispered, scolding himself under his breath.

Jozef finally saw the old man was human after all. 'You persuaded Gerhard to give up Jozef and then you murdered him at Hadamar.'

He knew, thought Michael. Jozef knew. But how? The professor. 'Nonsense,' he said, calmly trying to sweep the revelation off the table like bread crumbs.

'It was National Socialism policy to report and then murder physically and mentally handicapped children. It was your job to ensure that policy was executed accurately and efficiently.'

Michael's mind began to reel. He could see increasingly little room for manoeuvre. Then he smiled and regrouped. He finished his coffee and he enjoyed the warm sensation in his throat. Caffeine stimulated his brain. He leaned forward and Jozef focused, ready to hear his concession. Their heads came closer until their lips were almost touching, like lovers. Michael's face was suddenly bigger than the moon. The sunlight warming central Berlin was blocked out. There was only Michael's round features left. His eyes.

Michael's face then altered grotesquely and screwed up into a heated ball of hatred. Jozef recoiled but Michael's hand had a tight hold on his collar, throttling his attempt to retreat. He was hurting him. Jozef wanted to shout out, but he felt paralysed. He needed to get out of there. He needed to get out.

'I hate this country,' hissed Michael, spitting out words like blood. 'These people, this weakness. I am drowning. I can't stand it.'

Every syllable was soaked in poison. Jozef was forced to ingest every burning one. Those eyes.

'I must get out of this place, this Germany. I must be free. You are the key to my freedom, do you understand?'

Jozef still dare not move. All he could feel was Michael's choking hold on his collar.

'I need you to come to South America. You are my ticket. I am old. They want youth, a future. You represent the future Jozef.'

CHAPTER THIRTY-SEVEN

Catharina and Gerhard shared silence in their dining room as they thought about what they had done, all they were responsible for. Two people lay dead as a result of them.

Catharina felt sick. She climbed up off the floor. Her bruised knees cracked with numbness. She could not walk far and she still had to suffer *him* so close. She wanted to beat the life and the lies out of him, but she was exhausted. She did not have the heart anymore.

She hauled her wooden frame back into the chair she had sat in when Gerhard had first returned home from work. Gerhard remained huddled on the floor, like he needed permission to rise. The telephone rang loudly, rudely. Catharina jumped, but Gerhard did not flinch. She wanted to hurl it violently across the room and send it smashing through the window. But she did not and did not know why. She picked it up and enjoyed the normality of conversation.

'Mum, it's Jozef.'

'Jozef,' she said, trying to brighten up too quickly.

Jozef immediately sensed it. 'Are you okay?' he said.

'I'm fine darling. Long day. That's all.'

'Mum, can you and dad come and get me a day early? I don't want to wait until Saturday. I'm ready to come home now.'

'That might be difficult,' said Catharina, working through the consequences in her head. 'Everything is okay, isn't it? No trouble?'

'Fine, mum. Michael is here. He is hanging around. It's strange to be honest. I'd rather you came and got me tomorrow.'

Michael, she thought. Anger rushed through her blood again. 'Jozef, is everything alright? Michael hasn't hurt you has he – or threatened you?'

'No, no,' said Jozef, still fragile and bruised emotionally after the afternoon's disturbing encounter. 'Don't be silly,' he said, shielding his mother from the truth. 'Michael is our friend. Why would he hurt me?'

'I know, I know. I'm just being silly. You know me. We'll be there tomorrow, as soon as we can. Don't worry. We will be there.'

'Auf Wiedersehen Mutter,' said Jozef, allowing fear to creep into his tone.

'Auf Wiedersehen Jozef,' Catharina said. 'I love you. Auf Wiedersehen.'

Catharina placed the telephone calmly back down. She turned around to Gerhard. He still had not climbed up off the floor.

'What have you done now?' she said.

Catharina and Gerhard drove the 600 kilometres from their home in Munich to Berlin and Jozef overnight. Catharina could not sleep and Gerhard had no choice. It was time he did something for her. Now Gerhard was sleeping fitfully in the passenger seat. Catharina was to his left, driving. She was glad to. The act had proved difficult and stressful at first, but now she was smoothly flying along the anonymity of the *autobahn*. It was proving therapeutic.

Catharina found her thoughts like their car rolling through the dark. Headlights lit the way, but she could not see clearly. She liked it that way and had been happiest in her life when she had not looked too far forward. Appreciate what you have now, she had always told herself. Catharina had endured a lot, but less than most in the generation still reeling, still haunted by ghosts after the war. Yesterday was never far from today. Tomorrow always seemed distant.

Gerhard stirred and opened his eyes. They weighed heavy and were pained with a lack of deep sleep. Catharina flicked her look from the road to her right and her husband. He noticed, but did not say anything. He felt he was journeying with Heinrich Himmler himself and all the malevolent intent that entailed.

'Can you light me a cigarette?' she said. She could still only be cold and impolite.

'You don't smoke.'

'I feel like it tonight,' she said.

Gerhard reached into his jacket pocket and pulled out his cigarettes. He lit one and handed it to his wife. She took it and sucked on it, drawing a deep, heavenly drag. The nicotine floated high into her head and massaged it, filling it with fog. She felt good suddenly. Gerhard thought briefly about joining her, but then thought better of it.

He rolled over, rested his head uneasily against the car window and closed his eyes. He drifted in and out of half-sleep. He knew he was kidding his body, which was starting to ache from the long night and being unable to stretch out properly in bed. His eyelids hung like lead. The car smacked against a hole in the road. It jolted him and awoke him angrily. Catharina smiled at his misfortune and inhaled more of her cigarette. She felt adult.

She thought of Jozef, the son she had given birth to and who they had given to the Party to care for in 1944. Time had not allowed the moment or thought to heal. She swallowed a nauseating hatred. It felt in hindsight like tossing her baby into the jaws of a Great White. How naive she had been. But Gerhard had always known what the consequences were. He had known.

Catharina thought about crashing to her right and hurling Gerhard out into the night. Maybe he would survive; maybe he would not. He would have had more of a chance than Jozef. She had thought Jozef would return to them after the war. He would run giggling and laughing with his funny gait unbalanced. She had loved it and admired his bravery. Her little soldier. Toddling was doubly difficult for him to master. Still, he loved trying.

He would swing his little legs forward left, right, left, right. His condition made it look like he was cradling an invisible egg between them. Catharina would encourage him and hold out her hands, crouched down so their eyes danced in the same light. He would fall flat on his face and immediately pick himself up again. The smile never left him. She could not recall him crying then. He might have done at the end. The horrific idea poisoned her. She would never forgive herself for not being there for him. Catharina could have killed the doctor or nurse administering the lethal injection which murdered him and they could have all died together. She would have been happy then. She would have told Jozef that they were all going to sleep for a very long time. He would have liked that and nuzzled his head into her chest. She would have cried, but she would have accepted it with him close.

Real tears now trickled down Catharina's cheeks. She was tired. The nicotine high from her cigarette had worn off and she felt rising rage again. Catharina looked around them. No cars. She was going to do it. She was actually going to do it.

Catharina locked her left hand onto the steering wheel to hold the car steady and flung the rest of her frame violently to her right and reached across and banged Gerhard's door open. He lurched from his sleep. The wind whistled through the car, allowing the demons to enter and fly around their heads. Catharina was glad of their company.

Gerhard nightmarishly looked down at the tarmac racing by below at suicidal speed. He would be sliced to pieces. He swung himself back into the car and grabbed the door, which continued to flap and smack dangerously open. He banged it shut and the demons flying above them vanished into the night. Gerhard caught his breath and looked at Catharina. He looked scared. She did not care. She did not care anymore.

CHAPTER THIRTY-EIGHT

Catharina and Gerhard were stood at a safe distance, watching. Jozef had asked them to do that. He was meeting Michael at the train station. They were due to catch the 6pm from Berlin to Frankfurt. The station throbbed with people like ants, hurrying about their daily business with little thought for others. Jozef continually found himself repeating 'excuse me' and 'pardon me' while he weaved his way to a spot beneath a huge clock. It was 5.15pm. Jozef was due to meet Michael at 5.30pm.

Jozef found a tiny oasis among the crowds and was happy to place his heavy case on the floor for a moment. His arms had begun to ache. He could feel his body prickle with perspiration from the effort. A gentleman with too much baggage banged into Jozef and jolted him with the impact. The man mumbled an apology, but he did not mean it. Jozef could not make it out, but instinctively smiled back in forgiveness. The man did not reciprocate. He felt weak for a second and hated himself for it.

He caught sight of Catharina and then Gerhard. They made eye contact, reassuring each other momentarily before turning their gazes away again. Jozef checked his watch. 5.22pm. He had regained his breath. His hole of inactivity was being observed by the multitude racing around him in a whirlwind of worried faces and bags and children and mothers and deadlines. Train stations were like crossroads in life, Jozef thought. Everyone was rushing to get somewhere, but few seemed to be looking forward to the journey.

'Jozef,' said Michael, magically appearing before him.

He looked relaxed and in control. Jozef had tried to forget the unsettling ordeal that day in the café. Now he only found himself smiling submissively. Michael was dressed immaculately – white suit, matching white hat and deep brown shoes, which sparkled perfectly with polish. He had only a small suitcase, which Jozef thought strange to contain an entire lifetime, but there were things about Michael Jozef would never understand.

'Do you have your passport?'

'Yes,' said Jozef, unveiling it in his inside jacket pocket.

Michael was satisfied. 'Come. This is the start of something wonderful, a new life, a new adventure, a new beginning. For both of us. Great things await. Great things. But first, let us arrive there safely.'

Michael looked hurried for once, leading Jozef over to the platform for the 6pm for Frankfurt. Jozef was quietly terrified. He did not know how he was going to say it. Michael ruled him. He always had. Jozef could not go against him, not now, not ever. He fleetingly thought about slipping away, into the jostle of anonymity. He had his own life to live and who knew where that might lead?

'Here we are Jozef,' said Michael, as if his son needed regular, personal announcements. 'Platform 6 for the 6pm to Frankfurt. It is only 5.50pm. We are in good time. Perfect.'

'I'm not going,' said Jozef.

The words didn't feel like his when they dropped from his mouth. He had repeated them so often in restless dreams that now that he was really saying them they felt only more unreal. He sensed his spirit floating gently, safely above the bodies trapped together on the platform like sardines captured in a great net, struggling hopelessly against the inevitable.

'I'm not going Michael,' Jozef heard himself say again.

The words paralysed his father, who now stopped. He had heard them, but pretended not to have. This was not wholly unexpected, he thought. It was a big step.

'Come,' he said quickly, glazing over the revelation. 'Have you got your passport?'

'Michael, I am not going with you. I don't want to.'

Michael turned and looked at Jozef. He had to find the right response. He did not have much time. 'We have talked about this,' he began. He should have rehearsed this more thoroughly, he thought. 'I need you in Argentina. We need you. There is nothing for you here. Greatness awaits us both. Greatness.'

'Michael Drescher, Dr Michael Drescher,' said a voice.

Three policemen had turned up.

Jozef did not know what was happening.

'Yes, this is him,' said Michael. 'But I am afraid this will have to wait. I have an important meeting in Frankfurt. This is my train. I must be on it. Government business, you understand. Please telephone forward. They will verify who I am.'

'Dr Michael Drescher, we would like to question you about the murder of Januariusz Sobczak,' said the lead policeman, who was wearing a plain suit and was flanked by two subordinates in uniform. 'Do you understand sir?'

'Yes, yes, I understand perfectly,' said Michael, placing his case by his side and preparing to give himself up.

Jozef did not understand. He glanced up at Michael and felt like a small child. The years fell off his father. Michael's thinning, silver hair grew thicker and darker, echoing a youth not too short lived. His hands lost their aging grains and looked stronger again, ready to get to work.

The two officers in uniform struggled to get behind him. Michael had discreetly stepped back. No bystanders realised what they were witness to.

'You son of a whore,' muttered Michael bitterly under his breath.

Jozef struggled to comprehend Michael's last statement. He was too young to know what a whore was.

'I beg your pardon sir,' said the commanding officer.

'You son of a whore Jozef!' he cried and people nearby startled.

Michael flicked out a blade from the sleeve of his jacket and slashed the commanding officer across the throat. Blood flashed across Jozef's eyes, blinding him. Those around thought someone had spilt red paint.

Michael was gone, flying, bulldozing a trail through the crowd and onto the train. Blood was on his jacket and on his hands. His blade was still drawn.

One policeman stayed with his commanding officer while the other raced after Michael and saw him board the train. There was no time to tell staff at the station to delay it. The remaining officer tried to hold in the other man's throat, but it was hopeless. He was already choking. Blood was everywhere. A woman cried in horror.

Jozef was too stunned to move. What had just happened? He did not understand.

Catharina saw the commotion and immediately abandoned her post on the station bridge and raced through the throng. Jozef, she thought.

Michael saw a free seat in a carriage opposite a woman with two small children. He instinctively grabbed it. The woman was consumed by an infant, who she was impatiently trying to cradle to sleep. The other child watched Michael transfixed. Michael hastily tore off his bloody white jacket, shirt and hat, and bundled them into a pile beneath his seat. He pulled on a scruffy hat, one a poor factory worker might wear, and a thick jumper. He tilted the cap over his eyes before removing his shoes and his socks, adding them to the growing pile beneath his seat. The child continued staring, mesmerised. Michael noticed.

The policeman in pursuit arrived at the cabin.

'Have either of you seen a man in a white suit?' he asked hurriedly.

The woman with the crying toddler looked up. Her child had.

Michael looked at him, holding his eyes in his own with expert patience.

The child remained silent.

'Nein,' answered the lady, preoccupied with her children.

'Sir?' said the policeman.

Michael answered convolutedly in thick Polish. The policeman did not fully understand. He looked his appearance up and down, and stopped at his bare feet. Probably homeless and without a ticket, he safely assumed before quickly moving on. The older child was still staring. The woman did not understand Polish either, but she could pick it out in a crowd of millions. She had instinctively learnt to do that during the war. She was still afraid of Jews.

CHAPTER THIRTY-NINE

'I still wonder if that man on the train the police saw that day was my father,' said Jozef.

He had felt old this morning. Maybe that was a good thing, he thought, sat in front of a group of teenagers. He never envisioned grey hairs on his temples, creeping inexorably inwards like winter. They still did not look like his when he spied them in his reflection.

He was talking to a class of 30 students. He guessed they were fourteen or fifteen years old. He was not quite sure. The attractive female teacher had told Jozef what year they were in upon his arrival at the school, but the language did not mean anything to him. He mentally only dealt in old money.

'My name is Jozef Drescher. I was born on April 3, 1941,' he said, introducing himself.

He had grown into his new role, his new life, but he was still not entirely comfortable speaking publicly – it did not come naturally to him.

'I grew up in Munich believing my name was Jozef Diederich, born one month earlier on March 3, 1941. My parents, Gerhard and Catharina Diederich, adopted me in 1945, in the final days of the Second World War. My biological father was Dr Michael Drescher, who gave me to my parents to protect me from what was happening to so many children of leading Nazis at that time. My father did not want that for me. He wanted me to survive. He wanted us to survive and help start a Fourth Reich.'

The teenagers' faces looked repulsed at the thought of a Fourth Reich.

It was 1999. Jozef smiled to himself. He realised he must learn to hide his feelings better. This was a very serious subject after all.

'Did you ever find out who the real Jozef Diederich was?' one girl asked. She raised her hand almost after speaking.

Manners had changed, thought Jozef.

'Yes. He was born with cerebral palsy to my adopted parents. He was killed, the last child to be murdered by the Nazis as part of Hitler's policy of euthanasia of physically and mentally impaired children. Jozef Diederich died in Kaufbeuren-Irsee state hospital in Bavaria on May 29, 1945, three weeks after American soldiers had liberated the town. He was killed by lethal injection.'

The pretty teacher interrupted. 'We learn, Herr Drescher, how your father oversaw the murder of more than 10,000 physically and mentally disabled people at Hadamar, one of five killing centres the Nazis created to carry out Hitler's policy of euthanasia. How do you live with what your father did?'

'You can't live with it. What he did. Is the past always present? Can the future ever be free of guilt?' Jozef was only coming up with more questions. 'Why didn't others try and stop him? Why didn't my real mother try and stop him? I believe she covered her eyes to what was happening at Hadamar in 1941-42. She wanted to believe nothing was going on. That is my impression of her. I still see the hatred in my father's eyes. He was a monster, not all the time, but the monster was always there. He enjoyed what he did to those people. He took pleasure in it.'

'Where did his hatred come from?' asked the teacher, continuing to lead the debate from the other side of the classroom.

'Who knows?' said Jozef in his first unrehearsed answer of the morning. The questions were normally the same. 'My father hated weakness. He hated people showing emotion. He hated even himself when he did so. He had a cold nature. He showed warmth when he had to, but it was only a show. He had no real warmth. He never abandoned the ideology of the Nazis, even after the war. He continued to be a zealot. He believed in what Hitler did.'

'Do you look like him?' questioned one girl suddenly.

'No,' smiled Jozef, 'I don't look like him.'

The End

Dear Reader

I very much hope that you have enjoyed reading A Quiet Genocide.

You can make a big difference.

Reviews are the most powerful when it comes to getting attention for a book. Honest reviews of my book help me get more attention for what I write.

If you've enjoyed this WW2 novel I would be very grateful if you could spend a few minutes leaving a review (it can be as short as you like) on this novel's Amazon page.

Thanks a lot in advance, Glenn Bryant

ABOUT THE AUTHOR

Glenn Bryant grew up in Grimsby, the north of England and has a Masters degree from the University of Dundee, Scotland in modern history.

He trained in newspaper journalism and is a qualified and experienced senior journalist. *A Quiet Genocide* is his first novel.

FURTHER READING

In case you enjoyed reading *A Quiet Genocide*, you might be interested in reading some of our other titles.

Amsterdam Publishers specializes in WW2 historical fiction and in memoirs written by Holocaust survivors.

Please note: We always welcome new WW2 fiction manuscripts and manuscripts by Holocaust survivors.

You are invited to send them to info@amsterdampublishers.com.

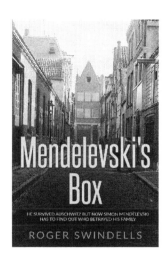

Mendelevski's Box, by Roger Swindells, is available as paperback
(ISBN 9789493056107) and ebook.

September 1945. Auschwitz survivor Simon Mendelevski, penniless and unkempt, returns to Amsterdam in a desperate search for his family, friends and neighbours. Simon meets two Dutch women, both of whom have also suffered. One, known to him before the war, is anxious to make amends for what she perceives as a failure by her fellow citizens to protect the Jewish population while easing the pain of her own loss. The other arrived in the city after the bombing of Rotterdam in May 1940 during which she lost a limb. He searches for the address where he and his Jewish family were hidden prior to their arrest by the Nazis for anything tangible connected to his family, and for whoever betrayed them. Only after finding answers can he start to rebuild his life.

175

The Time Between: Love, loyalty and betrayal in Nazi-occupied Amsterdam by Bryna Hellmann-Gillson.

This historical novel depicts three young Jewish women, Pam, Jo and Hannah, and their family and friends during the physically, psychologically and morally difficult years of the German occupation, 1940-1945. They print illegal newspapers and false documents, hide Jewish children, commit sabotage and murder.

Their lives come together through Adrian, a young man risking his life in the resistance. He is Pam's brother, Jo's first infatuation and Hannah's lover. "Isn't this the between time?" he asks. "One day real life stopped, when the Germans came, and some day real life will start again." For some of them, it did.

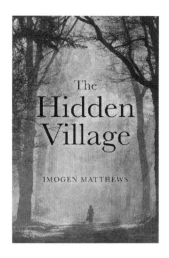

The Hidden Village by Imogen Matthews is available as Kindle ebook
audio and paperback (ISBN 9789492371256).

Deep in the Veluwe woods lies a secret that frustrates the Germans. Convinced that Jews are hiding close by they can find no proof. The secret is Berkenhout, a purpose-built village of huts sheltering dozens of persecuted people. Young tearaway Jan roams the woods looking for adventure and fallen pilots. His dream comes true when he stumbles across an American airman, Donald C. McDonald. But keeping him hidden sets off a disastrous chain of events. All it takes is one small fatal slip to change the course of all their lives for ever.

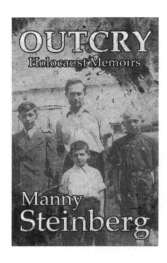

Outcry - Holocaust Memoirs by Manny Steinberg is available as paperback (ISBN 9789082103137) and Kindle eBook. This memoir has been published in English, French, German, Chinese, Italian and Czech.

Manny Steinberg (1925-2015) spent his teens in Nazi concentration camps in Germany, miraculously surviving while millions perished. This is his story. Born in the Jewish ghetto in Radom (Poland), Steinberg noticed that people of Jewish faith were increasingly being regarded as outsiders. In September 1939 the Nazis invaded, and the nightmare started. The city's Jewish population had no chance of escaping and was faced with starvation, torture, sexual abuse and ultimately deportation.

Outcry - Holocaust Memoirs is the candid account of a teenager who survived four Nazi camps: Dachau, Auschwitz, Vaihingen an der Enz, and Neckagerach.

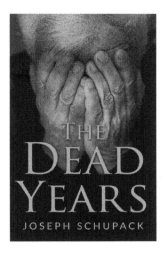

The Dead Years - Holocaust Memoirs by Joseph Schupack is available as paperback (ISBN 9789492371164) and as Kindle ebook. Also available in German as Tote Jahre.

In *The Dead Years*, Joseph Schupack (1922- 1989) describes his life in Radzyn-Podlaski, a typical Polish shtetl from where he was transported to the concentration camps of Treblinka, Majdanek, Auschwitz, Dora / Nordhausen and Bergen-Belsen during the Second World War. We witness how he struggled to remain true to his own standards of decency and being human. Considering the premeditated and systematic humiliation and brutality, it is a miracle that he survived and came to terms with his memories.

The Dead Years is different from most Holocaust survivor stories. Not only is it a testimony of the 1930s in Poland and life in the Nazi concentration camps - it also serves as a witness statement. This Holocaust book contains a wealth of information, including the names of people and places, for researchers and those interested in WW2, or coming from Radzyn-Podlaski and surroundings. The book takes us through Joseph Schupack's pre-war days, his work in the underground movement, and the murder of his parents, brothers, sister and friends.

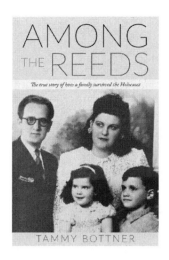

Among the Reeds: The true Story of how a Family survived the Holocaust by Tammy Bottner is available as paperback (ISBN 9789492371287) and as Kindle ebook.

Belgium, 1939. Melly Bottner is just eighteen with a three-week old newborn son when the Nazi occupation of Belgium begins. She and her young husband Genek live in fear as it becomes obvious that all Jews will soon be taken. Watching friends and neighbors disappear as the Germans carry out their shocking purge, the young family confronts an awful truth: if they are to survive, they must rip their own family into pieces.

In this biography from Melly's point of view, author and granddaughter Tammy Bottner delivers a true and moving family memoir. This meticulously written and researched account brings to life the horrific decisions Bottner's grandparents had to make simply to survive. Through their monumental choices, Tammy Bottner's grandparents ensured the survival of their family and made their post-war reunion possible.

Among the Reeds is a deeply personal family memoir that is part-biography, part psychological observation of the extraordinary wartime lives of a persecuted people. If you like true stories of courage, heart-stopping near misses, and tear-jerking choices, then you'll love Tammy Bottner's compelling account.

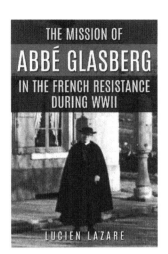

The Mission of Abbé Glasberg in the French Resistance during WWII by Lucien Lazare is available as paperback (ISBN 9781522840954) and as Kindle eBook.

The Mission of Abbé Glasberg is the fascinating story of a priest - of Jewish origins - who dedicated himself to the task of helping the refugees who were streaming into France during the years preceding World War II. Together with Father Chaillet, Abbé Glasberg created the ecumenical Amitié Chrétienne in May 1942 with the full support of Cardinal Gerlier, archbishop of Lyon.

Salo Muller

**See You Tonight
And Promise to Be a Good Boy!**
War Memories

*See You Tonight and Promise to be a Good Boy! War memories by
Salo Muller is available as paperback (ISBN 9789492371553) and
as Kindle ebook.*

'See you tonight, and promise to be a good boy!' were the last words his mother said to Salo Muller in 1942 when she took him to school in Amsterdam, right before she was deported to Auschwitz. She and her husband were arrested a few hours later and taken to Westerbork, from where they would later board the train that took them to Auschwitz.

The book is, in his own words, "the story of a little boy who experienced the most horrible things, but got through it somehow and ended up in a great place." Salo, at only 5 years old, spent his time during the Second World War in hiding, in as much as eight different locations in the Netherlands. The book tells the story of his experiences during ww2, but also explains how he tried to make sense of his life after the war, being a young orphan.

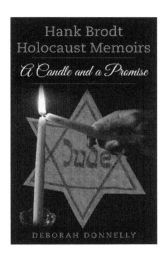

*Hank Brodt Holocaust Memoirs – A Candle and a Promise by
Deborah Donnelly is available as paperback (ISBN
9781537653488) and as eBook.*

A story of resilience, *Hank Brodt Holocaust Memoirs - A Candle and a Promise* makes the memories of Holocaust survivor Hank Brodt come alive. It offers a detailed historical account of being a Jewish teenager under the Nazi regime, shedding light on sickening truths in an honest, matter-of-fact way.

Hank Brodt lived through one of the darkest periods of human history and survived the devastation of World War II. Born in 1925 into a poor family in Boryslaw (Poland), he was placed in a Jewish orphanage. Losing his family when the Germans invaded Poland, he waged a daily battle to survive. Moving from forced labor camps to concentration camps, one of which features in Schindler's List, his world behind the barbed wire consisted of quiet resistance, invisible tears and silent cries for years on end.

Holocaust Memoirs of a Bergen-Belsen Survivor & Classmate of Anne Frank by Nanette Blitz Konig is available as paperback (ISBN 9789492371614) and as Kindle eBook.

In these compelling Holocaust memoirs, Nanette Blitz Konig relates her amazing story of survival during the Second World War when she, together with her family and millions of other Jews were imprisoned by the Nazi's with a minimum chance of survival. Nanette (b. 1929) was a classmate of Anne Frank in the Jewish Lyceum of Amsterdam. They met again in the Bergen-Belsen concentration camp shortly before Anne died.

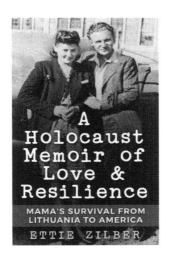

A Holocaust Memoir of Love & Resilience. Mama's survival from Lithuania to America by Ettie Zilber is available as paperback (ISBN 9789493056).

In her own words, Zlata Sidrer tells the story of how her life in Kaunas, Lithuania, changed forever with the Nazi occupation in 1940. Gone was her dream of becoming a doctor—instead she found herself trapped in the Ghetto along with the rest of the town's surviving Jewish population, before being transported to Stutthof Concentration Camp and eventually taken on the infamous Death March through the freezing Polish winter.

Rescued from the Ashes. The Diary of Leokadia Schmidt, Survivor of the Warsaw Ghetto is available as paperback (ISBN 9789493056060) and as Kindle eBook.

The diary of a young Jewish housewife who, together with her husband and five-month-old baby, fled the Warsaw ghetto at the last possible moment and survived the Holocaust hidden on the "Aryan" side of town in the loft of a run-down tinsmith's shed.

Made in the USA
Columbia, SC
22 October 2020